ROAD RAGE

Karina Kantas

Review Quotes

'This is my first time reading Karina Kantas, and I was not disappointed, this is a fast paced well written book. The world of powerful racing machines, MC gangs, violence and love, it has it all.'

'My first book by this author but definitely NOT my last! You've got the whole shebang - bike racing, hot guys, Outlaw MCs - and a female character that has gone through enough stuff in her before to not want anything to do with them again.
I liked Gem's character - she was strong, feisty, and made no apologies for her past.'

'I have to say I am very impressed.. the characters flowed and the story didn't stutter it was action packed and i loved watching the characters grow and mature.'

'If you love MC books you'll fall in love with this one, the characters, the story line and you won't want to put this book down. Absolutely loved it.'

'The story in this book draws you in, entwining you with the characters as each page is read. It is detailed and colourfully twisted to keep you on the edge of your seat. You really feel the pain of the main character and it envelopes you with emotion, as you hang on every last word.'

Table Of Contents

Rage
Hawks
Author's Note
More Titles

Rage

"Clean up in aisle six."

I was busy stocking up the shelf when the call rang out. A box of canned fruit sat at my feet. I turned and headed for the stock room to get the mop and bucket.

The ghastly green 'One Stop' smock hid the tight jeans and low-cut blouse I was wearing. Even though I had to cover up for work, I still wanted to look my best. Confidence was the key, so I thought.

The only time I struck up a conversation with customers was when I worked on the tills. And even then, it was just to comment on the weather or to ask after someone's health. So, when I turned into aisle six, I didn't pay much notice to the shoppers. My attention was fixed on the sticky, sweet-smelling goo lying across the length of the aisle.

"Shit," I said and tutted.

"Sorry about that," a husky male voice spoke.

There was laughter in his tone. I was about to apologise for my remark, but the words got stuck in my throat.

He stood staring at me with a wide grin that showed his perfect teeth. He was wearing racing colours; trousers: red with a white stripe. He held a helmet in the crook of his arm. Inside were bright coloured leather gloves.

"Not to worry," I said finally finding the words to speak.

Beaming a smile, he swept his hand through short, layered blond hair.

I couldn't tell what sort of build he had, as the padding in the protective clothing he was wearing would have built him up. However, from where I was standing, he was fit. Fit enough to get my interest.

My name was called over the speakers.

"Damn," I cursed. "I'm sorry, I have to go."

I placed the warning sign around the mess.

"It was nice to meet you, Gemma."

"The pleasure's all mine," I said. Then, regrettably, I walked away.

Before I turned from the aisle, I looked back and noticed the patch on the back of his jacket. Now the biker certainly had my interest.

I rushed up to the customers who were standing by the till, patiently waiting. Shoving the groceries into bags, I took no notice what or how I was packing. I wanted to get the queue down, get off the till, and go and take another look at the guy.

After the last customer left, I signed off, and then rushed to the toilets to check myself over. Reaching for my back pocket, I reapplied my coffee metallic lipstick, pulled the elastic band from my long brown hair. Combing my fingers through, I made sure I looked presentable. If my reflection looked this good in a cracked and rusty mirror, then I was sure to look okay on the shop floor under the artificial light. There was no way I was meeting the biker

Road Rage

again while wearing the smock. I didn't care what my supervisor thought. It wasn't very often that a male customer would catch my eye, but this guy was special.

I searched the aisles but couldn't see him. My misery started to peak as I thought I'd lost my chance, when my eye caught a glimpse of red from his trousers as he turned the corner. I found him beside the frozen food section. There were no other staff about, so I walked up to him and tapped him on the shoulder.

He turned around, startled, and then smiled when he saw me. I held my hand out.

"Hi, I'm Gem," I said and gave him my sexiest smile.

He shook my hand.

"Shep," he answered.

"Shep," I questioned. "Isn't that a name of a sheep dog?"

Luckily, he didn't take offence. He laughed and shook his head. "Long story short, my family lives on a farm; I got the nickname from the club."

"Yeah, I saw your jacket. So, you're a member of Rage?"

"I'm surprised you've heard of us. You don't look like the sort..." He stopped.

"It's okay. My leathers are out the back."

He laughed. "You in a club?"

"Nah, I just race sometimes. Down at the circuit."

"I've never seen you, pity," he said.

I stood staring at him, with a big grin on my face. I didn't care that I was probably embarrassing myself. I just couldn't turn away. After seconds of silence, awkwardness kicked in.

"I'd better let you get on with your shopping," I said. "Your food's gonna defrost before you get home. It was nice meeting you, Shep."

"You too, Gem."

"Maybe I'll see you around the circuit sometime."

"Hope so," he answered.

I expected him to give me his number, but it looked as

though my infatuation wasn't going to be returned. I turned and walked away, cursing myself, for being either too up front or too reserved. He's probably married, I told myself as I tried to come up with an excuse to why he wasn't interested in me. I knew it was probably the scar that ran down the side of my face that put him off. I felt I'd lost my facial attraction a long time ago. The war scar reminded me of a past I'd hoped to forget but got reminded of every time I looked in the mirror.

Dinner time came and I sat alone in the staff room on an old rickety chair. I was eating my pathetic, boring cheese and cucumber sandwiches and trying to block out the awful chart-topping number that was crackling away on a radio. Tracy, a fellow worker, came in swinging her hip, waving her hands and trying her hardest to hit the notes as loud as she could. I was about to cover my ears when she stopped and announced there was a guy outside asking for me.

My day turned sunny again when I saw Shep waiting outside the stairway door. But it was too sunny, and as I wasn't wearing my sunglasses, I had to cover my eyes from the glare.

"Hi," he grinned.

"Hey," I said and smiled.

"Umm. Listen, what time do you finish?"

"About five."

"Do you fancy going for a drink after work?"

"Sounds good," I grinned. Inside I was jumping up and down and my stomach was doing somersaults.

"You'll have to pick me up though. My ride is at home."

"Oh, what you got?" he asked.

"A Suzuki GSX R600."

His eyebrows rose. "Nice machine."

"And yours?" I asked.

"I've got a couple. I use the Honda VTR 1000 for the circuit. But I get around on my Yamaha R6, mostly."

"Cool. Bring a lid with you, okay?" I said, referring to a helmet.

Road Rage

"So, I'll see you at five?"

"Yeah, looking forward to it." I watched him walk away until a thought occurred.

"Hey, Shep." I called.

He turned.

"You married?"

"Hell no."

"See you later then," I smiled and pushed open the stairway door. I walked inside and leaned against the door and gave a lustful sigh.

I'd heard of Rage and seen them around, but I'd never associated with them before. Although the club had a good public image, there were whispers around the circuit. Other bike enthusiasts gave the Rage motorcycle club a wide berth.

It was amazing how three hours could drag. I was as nervous as a teenager who was about to pop her cherry. My anticipation made me feel young again. How should I behave? What was he expecting? What should I say to him? What can I ask? Why was I so bloody nervous? I felt Shep was special, and I wanted to make a good impression. I'd been alone for too long. Now it was time to get back out there and start dating again. One thing bothered me; I was planning on going out with a guy who lived the lifestyle I'd escaped from. Was I about to make yet another mistake?

Five o'clock finally came around, and I knew he'd be waiting outside for me. I was as excited to see his superbike as I was to see him again.

Shep was sitting on his machine waiting. And boy was it a beautiful piece of machinery, black with a bright orange stripe. The kind of bike you'd be able to see from down the bottom of a long road. It was obvious he looked after his bike. Most serious bike enthusiasts wouldn't leave their garages unless their machines were sparkling. I felt ashamed that my own ride was looking as though it just got back from a mud safari.

Wearing blue jeans and his Rage leather jacket, he gave me a sexy smile and then handed me a shiny black helmet with tinted visor. I zipped up my jacket, climbed onto the back of his bike, and leaned onto his back as we started off down the road.

It's almost impossible to talk while speeding on a bike, so I decided to leave the conversation until later.

We weren't having a particularly hot summer, but it was warm enough to enjoy whizzing down the motorway on the back of a bike. However, the trees, houses and towns continued to whizz by, and I wondered where the hell he was going.

He finally pulled into a retail park. The shops were closing but there were still plenty of things open. I wondered if we were going to the cinema or for a pizza or perhaps, he was taking me for a drink in The Layby, a classy bar I'd heard a lot about. Only I was surprised when he parked the bike outside the skating rink.

I took off the helmet, looked at Shep then back at the rink.

"Umm – where are we having this drink?" I asked.

"I thought we could have some fun while I get to know all about you. You up for it?"

"This will be interesting."

Fun. Yeah, probably be a lot of fun for him when he sees me falling flat on my arse and making a right fool of myself. I sighed and then followed him into the building. With the smouldering looks he'd been giving me, I needed to cool down.

It had been years since I skated, and as we queued up for the hired skates, my stomach churned from excitement.

"So, you done this before?" he asked as we laced up the boots.

I smirked. Well, yeah, I've been on lots of first dates before. "Not for a while I haven't."

"We'll take it slow," he promised with a smile.

I took his hand and he led me onto the rink. Immediately,

Road Rage

he started skating backwards while pulling me along.

"Fucking typical. Trust you to be good at skating," I gasped. That wasn't supposed to come out of my mouth.

"Been a while, but I used to come here a lot," he replied.

My confidence was shot. He probably wanted to speed skate around the rink, and here he was, stuck holding my hand. Yet, I was surprised how well I was doing. I'd yet to fall on my arse. It was coming back to me, and it wasn't long until we both picked up the pace.

"See?" he said. "It's like riding a bike."

"What kind?" I asked with a grin.

We talked about movies, music and motorbikes. Neither of us felt obligated to reveal everything.

It felt natural to chat and laugh with him, and when he twirled me around and held me tightly, it felt right.

I'd never been one for exercise, so after an hour or so, I started to tire and suggested we stop skating and have a hot chocolate in the cafeteria.

Time passed as we sat and talked. After the creamy chocolate, we shared a plate of chips covered with tomato sauce and slowly sipped Cokes. I couldn't decide whether it was Shep's shocking blue eyes or his cheeky, dimply smile that attracted me to him. Nevertheless, I was transfixed. His mouth opened and closed as he talked, but my mind blurred as I stared at his soft pink lips and watched his tongue dart out of his mouth every minute, a habit of his which I found endearing.

He chuckled at something he said, and so I gave a nervous laugh and then cursed myself for not paying attention.

"So, what was the last movie you saw?" I asked and then wanted to hide under the table for either going off topic or sounding immature.

Again, he swept his hand through his hair as he smiled and said. "What kind of stuff are you into? There's a thriller on at St John's Park if you fancy going with me."

My stomach jumped, and my heart picked up speed.

Yes, I silently yelled, a second date. I had pulled. I still had IT! I hoped I'd made a good impression on him. Okay, I didn't sit there and bat my eyelids, but I had been attentive and laughed at his jokes even though they weren't particularly funny. I admit, I played with a strand of my hair. Isn't that what you're supposed to do on dates? I'd been out of the game for too long and I'd never learnt the art of flirting. I was happy to be out on a date and having someone paying me a little attention after being invisible.

"Umm… yeah, sure that sounds good," I replied with a casual shrug, then added, "How about Friday?" It was a weird feeling; having something to look forward to. But I liked it.

For first dates, this one was exceptional, I thought, as I hugged onto his back on the ride home. I tried to visualise how the date would end. Would he peck me on the cheek before saying goodbye? Or should I invite him in for coffee and something more? No. I wasn't ready to go there just yet. I wasn't after casual sex.

I didn't trust him. Yes, I felt comfortable with him, but I knew he was a player. I knew from experience what dating a member of a motorcycle club was like. I wasn't sure if I wanted to go there again. But I felt sure Shep wasn't like that. It could all have been a ruse, but he acted sincere, so I was torn.

The date ended with more than a peck on the cheek, but we didn't go inside. We said our goodbyes beside his bike. I'd almost forgotten what a kiss and touch could do to your insides. Even though I ached for more, I stopped the embrace. After exchanging numbers, he promised to call. And although it was a line, I knew he would.

I never sat by the phone waiting for him to ring, However, I couldn't concentrate at work. I think I cleaned more jars off the floor than I put on the shelf.

Shep phoned two days later – keep a girl hanging, why don't you? He asked me out that evening and our dates continued every two days, but we never met up on weekends.

Road Rage

I knew he probably spent his time with Rage, and although it was early, I was worried that he didn't think I was good enough to introduce me to his friends. The sane half of me wanted to stay away from the club scene. The irrational half was itching to meet Rage and see what they were really all about.

At the ripe age of twenty-six, I was glad not to be single, but that didn't mean I thought of Shep as lifetime partner material. Sometimes you meet someone, and you have an immediate connection, and you just know. I knew that me and Shep weren't going to last. Yes, there was magic, sparks and such, and the sex was good. I just didn't see him as long term.

The Jester was Rage's local, as I discovered when he took me there one Friday night. When I saw the row of super bikes lined up outside the bar that was situated in the centre of town, my stomach flipped with anticipation. I was excited about meeting Rage, Shep's fellow racers and friends, but I was also worried. Was I dressed sexy enough to get attention? Did I have enough makeup on? Yes, I was being excessively vain; I just wanted to make a good first impression.

Shep took my hand and led me inside. I kept my head down and followed him to the bar. I felt eyes following me. I knew I was being scrutinised. Handing me a bottle of Bud, he then gestured to a table surrounded by seated bikers.

"Come on, there are some people I want you to meet."

"So, you're the mysterious woman," a dark haired, well-muscled guy said.

"Nothing mysterious about me," I replied. "What you see is what you get."

"Gem, this is Gbh, Doc, Turbo, and Blade," Shep said.

"Good names," I replied.

"Mine's legit," Doc said. "Not sure about this guy," he said, gesturing to the one called Gbh.

I laughed.

"So, you're a doctor?" I asked as I sat down on a chair beside Turbo and Doc.

"Yeah. I work down at the hospital."

"Good to know," I said.

"What do you do, Gem?" Doc asked.

I noticed the others listening, waiting for my answer.

"I'm working at 'One Stop' at the mo., just biding my time till something better comes along."

"Like what?" Doc asked.

"I'm an accountant," I answered.

"Good to know," the one called Blade said.

However, I wasn't about to tell them that I'd never worked as an accountant. As soon as I got my qualification, I left home with no money and no idea where I was going. At the time, I just had to get away.

Blade was well stocked. He wore his hair short, almost shaven, which gave him a hardened look. He demanded respect. I found out later that evening that he was the president of Rage.

Gbh had the muscles – probably where he got his nickname, I mused. Turbo was a lean black man. I assumed he got his name because of the speed when he raced. Blade - well that was one nickname that asked a lot of questions.

I met Pat and Bre later that evening. Pat was from Ireland and had a gorgeous accent. I could have listened to him talking all night. Bre was the only female member of Rage and, from the vibe she was giving off, she had no intention of welcoming another female to the club. She didn't even acknowledge me when Shep introduced us. She had glossy, blonde medium-length hair, a great figure, and her face was very pleasing to the eye.

The rest of the customers in the bar looked like regulars. Low rock music played in the background while chatter and the sound of cue sticks smashing onto the balls filled the room. If it wasn't for the cold shoulder I was getting, it would have been a warm atmosphere. The Jester was a

Road Rage

small but comfortable bar.

Club business wasn't discussed in front of me. In fact, what was said felt stilted. That was until bikes were mentioned; then the guys' eyes lit up, and you could see and feel the passion these guys had for their sport and lifestyle. Gbh's eyebrows rose when he learnt I was a biker and owned a Suzuki GSX. No one else talked to me. No one started a conversation with me. Doc was the only one who made any sort of effort. Even Shep ignored me most of the night.

I was thankful to leave the place.

"Not a friendly bunch, are they?" I said to Shep as we climbed onto the bike.

"You're an outsider. They're like that with everyone."

"What makes Rage so damn special?"

"We're the elite."

An arrogant answer, but it was the truth.

Rage was a closed group that didn't like strangers. They had money and didn't have a problem displaying that fact.

That night, I had a nightmare, and I didn't need a dreamer's dictionary to decipher what it meant.

It was dark, and only moonlight lit up the straight, empty road ahead. It was silent, complete silence. I felt I was walking on the edge of something. My feet were bare, and a chilled breeze bit through my pyjamas, and I had nothing but the urge to walk to keep me warm. I came to a crossroad. A large raven stood on a signpost and squawked loudly. The place names had been blackened out. The roads were only lit at the beginning; beyond was cloaked in utter blackness, as though those entered it would be swallowed up and never be seen again. Each path looked ominous, but I had to choose one. One led to freedom and happiness, the other - who knew, trouble, death or worse. There was a loud rumbling behind me, and I turned to see the road behind me crumble then disappear into nothingness. I started to run.

That's when I woke up. I knew what the dream meant.

It wasn't the first time I dreamt of the crossroads. I was going down the same road I'd travelled before, and at the end of the road, trouble was waiting. If I had any sense, I would end this relationship and my association with Rage. But, as my mother had told me time and time again, I had no sense. What I was doing was wrong and that was what the dream was telling me. But I was also being pulled to a place and situation where I felt free. A place I could be me again. My subconscious was warning me to walk away. I wore the leathers. I rode a motorcycle, but it wasn't enough. I needed the social connection, the brotherhood. I wanted to belong, and I believed Rage was a far cry from the Hawks; a different league, a club where I would be safe.

***

I arranged to meet Shep at the circuit. I didn't expect a welcome from the club, but that didn't stop me going over to their tent.

"Hi guys," I announced.

Startled faces turned my way, but they soon lost interest and turned back to their bikes. Only Doc bothered to greet me.

"Hey, Gem, what you doing here?"

"Racing. I like to take a spin now and again."

As no one else acknowledged my presence, I decided to leave.

"Good luck with the race, Doc."

"Yeah, you too." He smiled.

I kissed Shep and then walked away, back towards my bike station. I felt the tension leave my shoulders immediately. I don't need this shit, I silently cursed. There was no way in hell I was allowing Rage to ruin my moment. I needed to chill. My race was coming up.

I suited up and pushed my bike to the starting grid. As I sat waiting for the other bikes to get in line, my head turned, and I saw Rage's tent. The huge "Maxi" sponsorship banner was hard to miss. "Maxi" was a popular motor oil

Road Rage

and a perfect sponsor for Rage. No one was looking my way, which pissed me off. I opened the throttle of my bike enough to take off if the lights suddenly changed. To hell with them, I thought and turned my attention back to the track.

I was still on a high when I left the circuit. I had time to get home, shower and change before riding down to the Jester to meet Shep. I assumed the whole club would be there. However, only ten members were present.

It was a Friday night, and the pub was crowded. A rock band had set up a stage, left of the bar. I walked over to Rage and said hi. I ordered a beer and then looked around at the faces. Shep was absent. I suddenly felt uncomfortable, like I didn't belong. Even though I had every right to walk into the public bar and have a drink.

"Where's Shep?" I asked casually, as I leaned against the bar and grabbed a handful of peanuts from a dish.

"He'll be down later," Blade answered, and then turned his head away.

I munched on the salted nuts and silently cursed Blade for his abruptness.

A short blonde-haired woman who was sitting next to Pat turned my way and said, "Hey, you're Gem aren't you?"

I walked over to their table.

"I'm Dawn," she announced. "This is Tex."

I looked at the guy she was gesturing to. He had short black hair and was wearing blue jeans and the Rage leather jacket.

"You know my man Pat of course."

"You rode well today," Pat said.

I was surprised he saw me.

"Thanks."

"You been racing long?" Tex asked.

"A few years, but nothing serious. I get down to the circuit about four times a year. How long's Bre been racing for?" I asked as I lifted up my bottle in a toast to her.

She'd been standing at the bar throwing daggers my

way ever since I first arrived.

"A while. She's pretty good, don't you think?" Dawn said.

"Reckless more like," I answered, and then turned away. I could still feel her stare burning into my back. "She needs to have more control on the track. She's an aggressive rider."

Pat stared at me. I wasn't sure if it was because I insulted a member or because I sounded as though I knew what I was talking about.

"What were you doing with the novices? It's obvious you're a better rider than that," Tex asked.

"I like to win," I answered.

"Yeah, but wouldn't you prefer to win by beating someone better than you?"

I shrugged. "I suppose so. Maybe I'll move up next time I race."

We continued chatting about bikes and such, and then we moved from our seats to see the band better. By 10 o'clock the place was full. Tex hadn't left my side all night, although I never gave him any signs that I was interested. Dawn was nice. We had a laugh. It didn't seem as though she was scrutinising me like the others were. It was as though she'd accepted me for who I was.

Shep still hadn't arrived. I knew he wasn't coming. I finished my drink and headed for the toilets. As I walked inside, Bre was coming out. When she saw me, anger flickered in her eyes. She pulled me inside and slammed me against the wall.

"What the fuck's your problem?" I yelled.

"You're my problem," she answered, moving closer.

"I don't know what you're so worried about; I'm no competition."

I didn't know what I was defending myself for. I guess she didn't like it because I'd walked into her territory. There were plenty of hang-arounds and partners to the patched members, but Bre was the only racer.

"I know why you're here. I've seen it a million times," she

said quietly.

She was standing in front of me; I was backed against the wall and couldn't move. I didn't want to fight her. I wanted to talk this out. Find out what was bugging the woman.

"You want a bit. The club's name is seductive. It brings plenty of skanks to our doors."

She reached down with her left hand and grabbed my crotch.

"You're hot for the leather. I know what you want," she breathed huskily down my neck before her teeth nipped my skin.

"Get your fucking hands off me," I yelled, and tried to push her away.

Gripping both of my wrists with her left hand, she reached down and groped at my breast.

I struggled against her and cried out for her to stop. It wasn't until her hand tried to reach down into my jeans that the defence mechanism kicked in. My knee automatically came up and hammered into her stomach. Raising my right fist, I punched her in the face, knocking her to the ground. I then made my escape. I ran out of the toilets, straight into Tex.

"What's wrong?" he asked, as I pushed him aside and rushed into the bar, grabbed my helmet and jacket and headed for the door.

I knew he was following.

"Gem," he called.

"Leave me alone," I yelled, as I ran over towards my bike.

I brushed away the fallen tears. No man was going to see me cry. I felt his arms turn me around to face him.

"What's wrong?" he asked and stroked my face.

"Fucking Bre just came on to me in the toilets," I said.

He didn't look too surprised. "I'll talk to her. Don't worry she won't try that again."

He caressed my face again and lifted my chin up. "It's

because you're hot. You've got the whole of Rage turned on."

He laughed and I smiled.

"You do know how beautiful you are, don't you?" he said and then lent towards me and kissed my lips.

I tried to push him away, but he gripped me tighter and his kissing heated up.

I instinctively kneed him in the balls and then whacked him around the head with my helmet, which luckily, I'd been holding in my hand. He fell to the ground.

"Not you as well. I'm not some fucking club property," I yelled.

"Gem, wait," he shouted.

I ignored him and climbed onto my bike, hit the throttle and left a cloud of dust in my wake.

I didn't go to the Jester again for a couple of days. I gave Shep the excuse about being tired. I just couldn't bear the thought of facing Bre and Tex again. I knew I couldn't avoid the place for long, though. I never did tell Shep what happened that night. He had a short fuse, and I didn't want him starting a fight with one of his friends over me. Well, that was what any decent guy would do for his girlfriend. However, things didn't run that way in Rage, as I was to find out that evening.

After we got our drinks, we headed to where the others were seated.

"Hey," I greeted. I wasn't expecting an answer.

Blade indicated to Shep to leave. I was left alone with seven male members staring at me. It didn't go unnoticed that Bre wasn't present. I looked for her the minute I walked into the bar. I was secretly glad I didn't have to spend the night looking over my shoulder worrying what she was thinking or saying about me.

"So, where's Bre tonight?" I asked no one in particular.

"Yeah, about that," Blade said. His smile quickly changed into scorn. "You lay a hand on another patched member again, and you'll suffer a Rage beating. Do we understand each other?"

"If you're a hang around, property of the club, anyone can have you," Turbo said.

"No, they fucking can't," I yelled. "And God help them if they try."

I looked at each of their faces. They were serious. I wasn't about to push it or explain to them about being molested by two of their members. I doubted Blade would give a shit anyhow. I nodded my head and silently vowed that if another patch tried it on with me, I'd make sure I wouldn't walk away so easily.

"I'm gonna let that go for now, out of respect for Shep. But you're not a member of this club, and it's the first and only time I'm gonna be lenient."

Folding his arms, he stared hard into my face. I stared back. He didn't intimidate me.

"What we gonna do with you?" Turbo sighed.

"You want in?" Gbh asked.

I was shocked. That was the last thing I was expecting. I hadn't given it much thought up until then. I was happy enough hanging out with the club. I should have known hanging with them meant I'd become club property. I was Shep's girlfriend and happened to like riding fast bikes. I enjoyed being associated with their name, but I wasn't about to allow any female or male arsehole mess with me, whenever they felt like it. I'd rather walk away than go through that prospect stage again.

Blade didn't wait for an answer.

"To become a member of Rage, you need to own and be able to handle a super bike. We've seen what you're capable of, so you have that part covered."

Again, I was shocked. They had watched me race. I felt honoured that I'd finally gotten their attention.

"But you haven't been here long enough to bring anything into the club. Why should we allow you to join?"

"Membership is limited to those that we feel deserve the honour," Turbo added.

"And what's in it for me?" I asked.

Doc laughed and then replied. "Status, respect and money."

"Sounds good." I smiled.

"Okay," Blade said. "These are your options. You can either remain as a hang around or prove your worth."

"And how do I prove myself?"

"You and Bre have a problem with one another. If you're to be a member of this club, we need to get it fixed. I won't have any hostilities between members. You want in, you fight Bre one on one. You win. You get your patch. But I warn you, if you don't pull your weight, you'll be out. Decide now. You either stay and become Rage's property, you fight Bre, win and get your patch, or you walk away and don't show your face again."

"What's Shep say about this ultimatum?"

"He doesn't have a say," Doc barked.

"So, what are you gonna do?" Turbo asked.

"I'll fight," I said.

Blade nodded his head. "Be at my house at nine o'clock on Friday evening. Gbh will give you the address. I don't want to see you around here until then. You got it?"

"Yeah, I understand," I said, and then stood up while I waited for Gbh to write down Blade's address.

I found Shep leaning against the bar. He'd been watching the interaction.

"Take me home?" I said.

"Sure thing, let me speak with Blade first, okay?"

"Yeah. I'll meet you outside."

I left the bar without another word.

As I stood outside waiting for Shep, I lit up a cigarette and inhaled deeply. My mind was reeling. What the hell was I getting myself into? I'd already walked away from years of high status within a club, and now I was thinking about starting off at the bottom again. And although Rage was in a different league to the Hawks, I was surprised at how similar their club rules were.

Road Rage

Shit. And then there was the fight I had to contend with. I wasn't worried about going one on one with Bre. I was certain I could take her without too much effort. I doubt she had as much fighting experience as me. Only it had been a long time since I'd been involved in a serious brawl. And what was it Doc said I'd get in return? Status, respect and money. To be associated with Rage would be cool. Respect, well that was always a plus as long as that included respect from Rage. But where did the money factor come into it?

How much were these guys making on the races? I knew you could make good money racing professional, but it also took a lot of money to keep the club set up. Sponsorship would help. Even so, the money had to come from somewhere. In fact, it made me wonder just how many members actually came from rich families and which members made their money from Rage. Money was something I'd never had a lot of.

I'd already agreed to fight Bre, and that was going to happen whether I joined the club or not. I needed to get her off my back, and the bitch needed to be taught a lesson.

"Did you know that was going down tonight?" I asked Shep when we got back to my place.

"Yeah, I had a feeling. What did you expect, Gem? You slammed Tex down with your God damn lid, gave him a concussion for Christ's sake. You got off easy."

"The bastard tried it on with me," I yelled. "He practically raped me in the car park."

I saw Shep's fists clench. At last, some emotion.

"And" he said. "That still didn't give you the right to punch out two of our members."

The word 'our' made me step away from him. I was an outsider, even to Shep. I'd got it wrong. He had no intention of defending me.

"Will it get better?" I asked, my voice raising an octave. "If I join your club, will they finally respect me? Will you?"

Shep walked towards me and pulled me into his chest.

"I do respect you, Gem. But there is only so much I can do."

"What I don't understand is that they hate me, so why would they want me to join?"

"They don't hate you. I wouldn't be with you now if they felt that way. Shit, half of the guys fantasise daily about you. Blade's impressed with your riding skills and thinks you'll be a great asset. And I think you've made a friend for life with Dawn. Oh, and Doc's got it bad."

"What do you mean?"

"He really digs you. Can't you tell?"

I shrugged.

"And in answer to your question," he continued. "Yes, it will get better. For now, you're an outsider and Rage is wary of outsiders."

***

I was down at Blade's house at eight thirty, and I wasn't the only one who'd arrived early. There were at least eleven bikes parked on his gravelled drive.

Blade lived in the posh village of Brampton. The house boasted four bedrooms, a double garage and at least three other rooms, plenty of room for the parties I heard he held every week. Blade lived alone in the big house but had a cook working daily. He liked his luxuries and didn't have a problem showing off his wealth. I wondered how he could afford two cars, one being a Mercedes as well as four, show-stopping road bikes, just from his salary as an insurance salesman. I assumed he was either very good at his job or had a wealthy family. I thought it was likely the last, as most of Rage seemed to be loaded.

Lifting the brass knocker, I rapped loudly. Turbo opened the door to me. No greeting, just gestured for me to go inside. A Metallica song was playing in the background. I smiled; I didn't take Blade as an opera loving man.

The only member of Rage that attempted a respectful

hello was Doc. He greeted me, and then took me into the lounge and got me a drink.

I knew I'd need a least three or four drinks before I faced Bre. It wasn't that I was worried about the pending fight. I'd been in a few bar fights before, involving male and female opponents. I could take care of myself. No, it wasn't fear that was pumping through me. It was adrenaline and I always felt this way before a brawl.

The house smelt of fresh flowers, but I didn't see any around. Blade liked his plants; most of the sun-house was covered with them. The lounge was decorated cream and brown. I ran my fingers along the soft suede of the cream couch. I wasn't sure what type of wood his furniture was made of, but it looked expensive. The walls were painted cream and had white plaster designs running across them. A glass, sparkling chandelier finished off the exquisite room. To the right of the lounge was an open plan kitchen. All mod cons. Stylish red appliances and black gleaming marble work tops, and as with the rest of the house, it looked new.. I came to the conclusion that he must hire a cleaner; no way could a man keep a house that size so clean.

Blade came into the room and saw me talking to Doc. He acknowledged me by raising his bottle. I nodded to him.

Shep walked in soon after. He kissed me, made some small talk, and then I was left to my thoughts. I was glad as I wanted to be left alone.

As the clock ticked by, the rest of the club arrived. I thought back to the incident in the toilets when Bre assaulted me. Rage, intense anger was the only way I was going to come out on top. I had a good reason to pound her face in, and I was looking forward to it.

It was hard not to notice the glances and stares from the members as I stood alone by the door. I answered them with a smile or raised my glass, but the attention was starting to get to me. I recognised the faces, even though I didn't know all their names. The music volume had increased as did the conversation. I couldn't think straight. I needed some ME time, so I stood up and left by the back door. It wasn't just a back yard; it was an acre of ground, which included a swimming pool, sun house and two more garages.

I was standing outside, looking at the lights in the swimming pool, and smoking a joint when Shep found me.

"Wondered where you got to," he said.

"Didn't think I'd chicken out, did ya?"

"You okay?"

"I'm fine, just chilling," I answered and offered him the joint.

He took a deep drag and held it in before saying. "Just think, you'll be an official member after tonight."

I looked him in the eyes. "You think?"

"I've no doubt," he smiled.

"And then I'm untouchable," I said.

"Not to me you're not."

He pushed my body against his and kissed me fervently. I gave my desire back, but our moment was cut short when Turbo came outside and announced it was show time.

I inhaled the last of the joint before throwing it to the ground and grinding it with my foot.

My heart was pounding as I watched the club piling out of the patio doors and into the back. They looked eager.

Every muscle in my body tensed when I saw Bre. She was laughing at something Blade said. She looked relaxed and not tense and wired like I felt. Jealousy flowed through me. She was liked and even loved by the club, and I hoped I'd have the chance to earn the same respect.

Walking into the centre of the grassed garden, she took her jacket off and gave it to Tex. I followed suit, taking my jacket off. I laid it on a patio chair and then walked over to Bre. I knew Shep was following behind. The bikers circled around us, and then Blade stepped forward.

Road Rage

"Fight ends when one of you calls out a submission. No weapons, only skin."

"Whatever." I shrugged.

Reaching into my back pocket I pulled out my knife and handed it to Blade.

A few members looked surprised that I was carrying a weapon. But I learnt from experience. I wasn't about to walk into a fight without expecting the unexpected.

In normal circumstances, you verbally spar with your opponent before throwing the first punch. However, this was a test, and I needed to be careful what came out of my mouth. If everything went to plan, we would both be members of the same club, and I didn't want there to be any hostility between us. For now, I couldn't stand the bitch, and it was payback time.

"You can take the first swing," she said.

"Gladly," I replied and belted her in the mouth.

My fist had been clenched for the last five minutes. The rage had flowed down my arm, and spread through my knuckles. The force was enough to lift her off her feet and split her lip open. She retaliated by punching me in the stomach. Soon our fists were punching and pounding into one another.

Within five minutes, we were both exhausted and trying to catch our breath. My knuckles were bleeding, but I'd only just started. After another round, my left eye was swollen shut and my nose bleeding. I couldn't stand up straight as her punches had cracked a rib or two. I was hurting.

I was bent over, spitting blood on the ground when Bre shouted out. "You had enough yet? Submit and it's over."

Lifting my head, I strained to see her face. She had a bad cut above her left eyebrow, leaving her face streaked with dry and flowing blood. Her right eye and cheek were swelling, and I watched her blink as she strained to see me. I thought she'd made a big mistake wearing white in a fight. Her t-shirt was coloured in bright, fresh blood. She looked a mess, and I knew she was hurting as much as I was.

"Is that all you've got?" I called.

She rushed at me and floored me with one punch. I was dazed, maybe even knocked out for a few moments, but when I came to, I turned and saw her limping towards Blade. I shook my head hoping to clear the fuzz. Gingerly, I pushed myself off the grass. I couldn't balance on two feet and wobbled around while trying to focus on her. I heard an intake of breath and astonished gasps from the crowd.

Bre spun around with a look of surprise etched on her face. Shep shook his head, bewildered.

"You give," I yelled, and then coughed up more blood.

Blade stepped away from Bre. The fight was still on.

"You've got to be joking," she answered. "Don't you know when to quit?"

"I ain't finished," I called back.

A mixture of blood and spittle ran down my chin. I wiped it away with my arm and attempted to stand up straight.

Slowly, she walked over to me. I waited until she was close, and then in one movement, crouched down and swept my foot out, catching Bre's leg. She fell crashing onto her back. I crawled over to her and used the last of my strength to punch her in the face. This wasn't going to plan. I didn't expect Bre to be such a good fighter, and I never thought the fight would last so long. I knew I couldn't take much more. I was out of practice and definitely unfit.

She kicked me off and then stood up and booted me in the ribs.

I lay in a foetal position on the ground and held onto my stomach, wishing the pain away. However, the pain increased and evolved into the worst migraine I've ever experienced. I thought my head was going to explode. Squeezing my eyes shut, I then turned my head and vomited. Being sick helped ease the migraine. Breathing was difficult and only short gasping pants regulated it. When I was stable, I pushed myself off the ground and sat up to look for Bre. I

Road Rage

knew I wouldn't be able to stand. I had never submitted to a fight before no matter what shape I was in. I wasn't about to give in.

"Hell no," she gasped when she saw me. "Blade, if that bitch can take a beating like this, she deserves to be in the club."

Applause and a roar of approval drowned out my own scream of celebration.

Doc rushed over to me. "Come on; let's get you to a hospital," he said as he picked me up in his arms.

We made our way through the crowd with shouts of welcome and hollers. My head felt like it was splitting in two. I blanked out even before we'd made it inside.

I woke up as they were putting me on a stretcher outside the hospital. Thankfully, Doc took care of my injuries, so I wasn't bothered with routine questions such as why I was messed up. As well as bruising and cuts over my arms, I had two cracked ribs and concussion.

Doc stayed by my side until Shep showed up.

I was resting on the bed, with my ribs strapped up, when Bre came in the room. Her facial cuts had been stitched and dressed but her face still looked a mess. Shep got off his seat and walked outside, but not before giving Bre a sisterly hug.

"How you doing?" she asked me.

"Okay, and you?"

"I'll live," she grinned.

"Did Doc fix you up as well?" I asked.

"Yeah."

"He's a nice guy."

"Not my type," she answered with a shrug.

Bre sat in the vacant chair, but couldn't get comfortable, and so stood up instead. I could see she was hurting.

Holding her hand out, she smiled. "No hard feelings?"

I smiled back and we shook hands.

"Welcome to the club. Blade wants to know what size jacket to order."

"Twelve," I replied.

"Better make it a fourteen. You'll be doing a lot of racing and will need room to move. Listen, do you need anything?"

"No, I'm fine. Doc said I can leave soon, but I've got to rest up for a couple of days."

"Yeah, he said the same thing to me. I guess it's gonna be a while until we're riding again."

We laughed. It hurt. Tears streaked down our faces as we watched each others pain.

"You put up a good fight," Bre said once she'd calmed down. "It makes a change to have a challenging opponent. You're tough, and that's what Rage needs."

I smiled.

"You know, Blade noticed that you're not just experienced with a bike. You've used your fists a few times. Is there something we should know?"

I watched her scrutiny and decided to give her a ten second rundown of my past.

"Rage isn't the first MC I've been a member of, and those bikers were in a different league to you lot."

Bre quickly caught on. Eyebrows raised; she shook her head. "Don't think we're that different, Gem. You've a lot to learn."

She stood up and walked to the door. "See you later."

"Yeah, take it easy," I called.

I spent the next hour thinking about her cryptic statement. Was there some truth behind the rumours about Rage? Were these boy racers more than a clean-cut motorcycle club? And even if they were involved in illegal activities, how bad could it be? I'd done my share. I was no angel, but I'd left that life behind, and I didn't particularly want to go back to it.

Rage had a good name, and it would be cool to be associated with them. Plus, it meant I could be with Shep without any fear of the others. Still, after what Bre said, I wondered how legit the club was, and if I was getting in over my head.

Road Rage

While I was recuperating from the fight, Shep took me to my first street gathering. Although I'd recently heard about the illegal road racing that went on, I'd never been to a meet before. I was surprised how official and organised it was. There were about fifty or more bikers present, a colourful display of super bikes, and everyone seemed to know each other.

They acted like a family, even though there were at least five different clubs present.

There was an amazing party atmosphere, and I was proud to be associated with Rage, who were greeted with honour. Even though I arrived on the back of a patched member's bike, I wasn't wearing colours. I was still an outsider, and so I wasn't officially introduced to anyone, but that didn't worry me. I was too caught up with the warm and exciting ambience. Apparently, this was a small meet, and I was anxious to see what a large meet would be like.

Blade and Shep won their races, and I saw a roll of money exchanging hands.

The meet ended as quickly as it began; from an empty road, to a street full of bikes and spectators, and then the road promptly emptied again. I wondered how they got away with it. Where were the police? After the bikers split up, most met up again in different bars around the town to continue their legal partying.

Shep took me down to the Jester a couple of times that week, and although there were pleasantries, no one mentioned me patching in. It wasn't until Friday evening that I received a call from Turbo, instructing me to go down to Blade's house and pick up my colours.

I didn't realise all the clubs' officers would be there waiting for me, so I was surprised when I saw their bikes parked on the drive beside Blade's garage.

I parked my bike beside the others and shut off the engine. I left my helmet sitting on the seat and then walked up the steps to Blade's large mahogany door.

Turbo answered the bell. Standing aside, he gestured for me to go inside.

I stood by the coat stand waiting for Turbo to lead the way. I'd only been in the house once, and so I didn't know my way around. There were doors leading everywhere, and I had no idea which room the meeting was going to be held in. I undid the zipper of my jacket and then followed Turbo through the house.

Blade, Doc, Gbh, Pat and Dawn were sitting on the sofa when I arrived. Dawn asked me if I wanted a drink, as Gbh gestured for me to sit. I took the chair opposite them, thanked Dawn for the beer, and then took my jacket off and waited. She left the room, and I was alone, facing the officers of Rage.

"You need to answer some questions before you can be patched in," Blade said.

He was sitting on the sofa, his arms folded, giving attitude as he always did when we spoke.

"Be honest, cause we've already done our background checks, so we'll know if you're lying," Gbh informed me.

I shifted in my chair. I wasn't ready for an interrogation, but I understood their need for answers.

The first round of questions they fired at me were routine: family, school background and employment record. Then they asked me what bikes I'd owned or ridden.

"I had a Yamaha 125 at college, and then I owned a Harley Softail Crossbones," I answered.

They didn't look too surprised when I mentioned the Harley Davidson.

"I can handle any bike from a 125 up to 1000. As you know, I have a Suzuki GSX R600, and a Kawasaki 250, but would I'd like to own, if I ever win the lottery, is a Ducati." I grinned but it wasn't returned.

I knew what the next question was going to be, and my mouth dried up at the prospect of answering it.

"Have you ever been a member of any other motorcycle club?" Turbo asked.

Road Rage

This was a part of my past that I hoped to forget. I stared into Turbo's face. Doc nodded his head urging me to answer.

"Yes. I used to ride with the Hawks."

The name was not unknown to them. Blade's eyes lit. Doc smiled, but Turbo and Gbh looked uncomfortable with the news.

"How long were you a member?" Turbo asked.

"Three years. Listen, mind if I smoke?"

"Go ahead," Blade answered.

I pulled the packet of cigarettes out of my jacket pocket. My hands were shaking. I hoped the others didn't notice. I cupped my hands and lit my cigarette, inhaling deeply, glad for the burning taste.

"Do you still associate with them?" Gbh asked.

I shook my head. "No, I haven't seen a Hawk since I left the club a year and a half ago."

The chapter of the Hawks I used to run with was based in the South. I made sure our paths didn't cross.

"And you were a full patch?" Pat asked.

"Women aren't allowed to wear the wings, but I had the Lady tag, so yes, I was a full member."

"So, you were involved with their illegal activities?" Blade asked, leaning forward in anticipation of my answer.

"I was involved, yes," I answered defensively. "Look, that was a long time ago. I'm out of the game now. You needn't worry about the Hawks."

"We're not worried," Gbh said.

"I want a copy of your birth certificate and driving license to me by the end of this weekend," Blade said.

"Okay." I reached over and took the book Doc was holding out to me.

"Here's our code. Read it, memorise it then give it back to me next week," he said.

I was surprised Rage had a code. The Hawks had their own rules of conduct and such, but they were a seventy full-patched member club. Rage had only seventeen fully patched members, so I was interested to see what their club rules were.

"Welcome to Rage," Blade said and held out my new black padded leather jacket.

I held it up and gazed at the Rage logo. Two < symbols, one small and one large, both sat on the left and right side of a large, white letter R. The letters MC were embroidered underneath.

I put on the jacket and then spun around.

"How do I look?" I asked.

"You look good, Gem," Doc said.

The others at least made an effort to smile.

"We're having a party here tonight, an official welcome to the club," Blade said.

"Great. What time should I arrive?"

"Best for the guest to be late. Say around nine."

"Sounds good."

I shook hands with the officers and then left the room.

It was certainly a different patching in to the one I had with the Hawks. I didn't feel any pride. I didn't feel welcomed. They didn't trust me and I'd yet to prove my worth.

The night I became a patched Hawk was the happiest experiences I'd ever had. In a strange way, I was loved and respected by my brothers and sisters, and we partied and drank throughout the night. However, this patching in didn't have the same atmosphere. At least Blade had used caterers. The food was good. Mini quiches and gourmet sandwiches and other small finger foods. I scoffed, drank a couple of beers, and then decided to leave. There was nothing to keep me there.

***

I was too comfortable. I knew things were going to turn to shit. I was just waiting for the moment.

It surprised me that it was Shep that threw the spanner in the works. Until then, he'd been a passionate lover, a good friend and great company to be around, although

Road Rage

after he moved in with me, I noticed his mood swings. I knew when to leave him alone and when he wanted to talk. I'd only have to look at his face when he walked through the door to know what kind of mood, he was in.

We were hanging in the Jester, playing pool and just chilling. Shep had been acting up again, and so I kept my distance, as did the rest of the club. Two customers started arguing loudly. Then the row became violent, and fists started flying.

Rage stood on the side-lines and watched. I was leaning against the bar chatting with Dawn, when she suddenly stepped away in time; unfortunately, I got a fist in my face. I know it was an accident, I just got in the way, but that didn't stop Rage from jumping the guy.

One major code between bikers is to look out for one another. If an outsider picks a fight with a patch, they pick a fight with the whole club. And as I found out, Rage was no exception.

Bre helped me off the floor and asked if I was okay. I didn't answer. I couldn't take my eyes off Shep, who was pounding the guy's face in. Rage was watching and didn't make any attempt to restrain him.

As I went over, Bre held onto my arm. I shrugged her off.

"Shep, leave him alone. It was an accident," I yelled.

Shep turned around and slapped me across my face. I fell against a stool. Turbo came over and grabbed my arm.

"Leave it, Gem," he warned.

I ignored him.

"For fuck's sake. What the fuck's wrong with you?"

Turbo still had my arm in a tight grip when Shep rushed at me. I couldn't move. I saw him raise his clenched fist. I don't remember the rest.

I came to, disorientated. It wasn't until I heard Doc's soothing voice that I remembered what happened. Shep had hit me and not just once.

Doc saw the fear. "It's okay, Gem, he's not here. He's

sleeping it off."

"Not at my fucking house, he isn't."

"He's staying with a brother," Doc told me gently.

"What the hell is wrong with that guy?" I said, rubbing my bruising jaw.

"He'd been doing speed most of the night. I thought you knew. Speed always turns him violent."

"No. I didn't know," I said, feeling stupid that I was living with a junkie and didn't even know it.

"You just need to know when to stay away from him."

"Yeah, that's what Turbo said. I think he was trying to warn me."

Doc helped me off the floor, and I sat on a chair and downed the brandy Bre held out to me.

"So, what's going to happen now?" I asked.

"With what?" Doc asked, confused.

"With Shep beating up on me. What's Rage gonna do about it?"

Bre walked away, leaving me and Doc alone.

"Nothing," he said.

"You what!" I glared back at him. "You telling me, he can slap me around whenever he likes, and nothing is gonna be done about it?"

Doc shrugged.

"Well, don't expect me to lie down and take it," I yelled.

Chatter in the pub stopped.

"Jesus Christ! What the fuck is this, Doc? A member of the public accidentally punches a female patch, and so the club kicks the shit out of him, but it's okay for the boyfriend to pound his fist into the bitch's face, in front of the club? Is that what I am, Shep's bitch? Is that all I'm worth?"

Doc didn't have to say anything. Just having him holding my hand was enough. I was hurt, embarrassed and angry, and I felt my emotions about to pour out.

"I thought you guys were different, but you're just like the animals that I escaped from." I got up and rushed out of the bar.

Road Rage

I made Shep go down on his knees and grovel for forgiveness before I allowed him back into my life. He couldn't even remember the fight, let alone belting me. I told him he should stop using speed if he couldn't control himself, but he assured me that it was under control. I knew it didn't matter how much I badgered him about his intake. He wasn't going to stop. He was hooked. I just made sure I wasn't near him when he was on the stuff.

***

I was one of the Elite now, and I knew it wouldn't be long until I was called out to face my first illegal road race. I wouldn't be racing against another club. No. Blade wanted me to go against an outsider; one of those bike enthusiasts who sits by the window waiting for a sign that a race was on. Then he'd stand on the side lines watching and thinking he was hot shit and how he could take on any one of us racers and win. Well, Blade was gonna give one lucky guy his shot. No one knew who I was, so it would be a challenge for an outsider to get the chance to take on a member of Rage. Blade made his feelings known. I was not to lose. I had to prove to Rage, myself and any other contenders that I was the one to watch.

Boy, did I feel the pressure. If it didn't go to plan, and I didn't win, bang goes my reputation, probably my patch and certainly Rage's reputation as winners.

A week later, I finally got called out.

"You're racing next week," Blade told me.

My heart thumped.

"And make sure you buy some new leathers."

He walked off before I could tell him where to stick his order. I guess my regular racing attire wasn't good enough for Rage. I couldn't afford to buy a new outfit. Luckily, I didn't need to mention that fact to Shep. He understood the situation and took me shopping the next day. Shep chose for me a white racing suit with a blue stripe. I'd never worn a one piece before. It felt stiff and uncomfortable.

However, he said it looked good, and that I'd get used to it. My new helmet was dark blue as were my leather gloves.

The next few times I took the bike out for a run, I wore my new leathers as they needed to stretch before I could race.

***

Gbh phoned me and told me to meet the club at the Jester and to dress in racing attire. I didn't question his order. Something was going down that night, and I was eager to find out what. This was one time I wouldn't have refused a joint. However, Blade was adamant his riders had to be sharp and alert before a race, which meant no alcohol either.

I used straighteners on my hair and gave myself a quick manicure. Even though I'd be wearing gloves, I wanted to feel as though I'd made an effort. With the late notice, the race just hours away, I didn't have the time to get to the salon. I soaked in a relaxing bubble bath and sipped chilled white wine. To hell with Blade's order, I thought.

Shep came home with takeaway, so I didn't have to cook that night. I felt relaxed when we left the house, but nerves kicked into gear as we approached the pub. The super bikes were parked around the back so as not to cause unwanted attention. These were the best in their class, and it took money and time to keep them looking good. But boy, tonight, they looked as though they'd come straight out of a show room: waxed, polished, sparkling chrome and plastic. Shep had made sure I polished my bike. I wasn't about to let the club down.

I walked into the pub to find the whole of the club there. All were dressed in racing leathers. Everywhere I looked, vibrant coloured leathers and shiny helmets hit my eyes. The atmosphere was bubbling. Excited laughter and chatter mixed with a low volume of rock music. I felt proud to be part of it and to stand with my brothers.

Blade waved me over to where he was standing with Shep, Turbo and Doc; they had serious expressions on their faces.

"So, you ready to show Rage what you can do?" Blade asked.

"Yep. Where are we racing?" I asked.

Doc shrugged. "No one knows. We're just waiting for a call."

"You're a new face. No one knows how good you are, and I'm going to use that fact to make some money," Blade announced.

"You win the race you get ten percent," Shep explained.

"And what happens if I lose?" I asked.

"You won't," barked Blade.

I nodded my head.

"Tonight, you're gonna see what Rage is all about," Blade said.

His phone rang and we all waited with anticipation. I wondered how much money I could make that night.

He closed his mobile and shouted over the din, "It's on. Let's ride."

I started walking out with the rest of the club when Doc pulled me aside.

"Follow Shep; he knows where to meet up. It causes too much attention if we ride out of town together. We arrive as one unit. You ride at the rear, park up with the rest of us and stay by your bike until you're called."

It was my first time participating in an illegal road race, and I was nervous. "What about the police? What do I do if they turn up?"

"We've got marshals looking out for the cops. If they show up, you split. Go home. Someone will call you."

The beautiful machines pulled out of the car park in a sea of colour. The perfect sound of grinding and screaming revs filled up the street. Blade was the only member who wasn't riding his bike. His Aprilia was loaded on a trailer behind his Renault Megane. Dawn sat in the passenger seat.

Shep passed by me. He looked cool sitting on his Yamaha in a black racing suit with orange stripes. I saluted Bre as she flashed the lights on her green Ninja.

We kept a slow pace through the town, and my Suzuki was itching to be set free. "Soon, Baby," I soothed.

Shep knew where we were going. I obediently followed.

There was a big difference between watching a street race and participating in one. I was wearing the Rage colours. People now regarded me, and I was followed and scrutinised everywhere I went. I didn't care. I loved the attention.

The Hawks were regarded out of fear. Rage was respected for their talent. I was proud to be a member of the club.

After riding slowly through a sea of spectators and racers, we parked up and mingled as we checked out the competition. Shep, as usual, had his arm hanging over my shoulder, making sure all the hot guys in the vicinity knew I was taken.

There were a lot of smart looking bikes on display. Bikes were spray painted every colour imaginable. Half of them were show bikes; the kind that would never be ridden flat out, the owners too scared to damage their precious cargo. I didn't blame them. There wasn't one bike on show that wouldn't set you back less than twelve thousand pounds. The other colourful bikes were the racers.

We had an unusual rule in our gathering. Anyone found using a NOS (Nitrous Oxide System) was booed out of the streets. To me, it seemed unfair to race against a faster bike, but that was where the talent of the rider came in.

I'd done plenty of practice races with Rage, and Blade taught me how to zone in, forget everything around me and just picture the road and finish line. Zoning in was not as easy as it sounded. It needed a lot of concentration to

Road Rage

blur out the edges of the road.

Blade left our circle to set up a race for me. Some of Rage wandered off. I stayed glued to Shep. Most of the eager audience either had a bottle or a plastic cup in their hands. There was plenty of beer flowing. Shep took a bottle when offered. It was okay for him. He wasn't racing.

I stood with Shep at the finish line and watched Pat's front wheel cross first. Cheers erupted, but Rage was above that. Shep punched his fist in the air, and I clapped then went over to congratulate him. It was an easy win, and Pat wasn't making a big deal about it.

"Gem, you're racing next," Blade announced.

"Who's she up against?" Tex asked.

"The tosser on the blue and yellow Suzuki."

Everyone turned their heads to see the guy sitting on his bike, spit polishing his helmet. Turbo sniggered.

"He's got a faster bike," I moaned.

"I don't doubt your skill," Blade glared.

I sat on the start line and zipped up my jacket.

"I hear this is your first race," my opponent said.

"Is that why you took up the challenge? You think I'm an easy win?" I laughed hard, glaring at him, trying to psyche him out. He quickly turned away.

I was putting on my racing gloves when Doc came over.

"I've seen this guy race. Take up the middle and keep him on the right-hand side, he's a nervous rider. He'll slow the bike."

I nodded and put my helmet on. Taking a deep breath, I visualised the finish line until the edges of the road began to blur.

His bike left the starting line before mine, but I soon caught up with him. I took Doc's advice and edged him to the side of the road. He immediately eased off the throttle. I wasn't sure if I should make it look too easy, especially as it was my first race, so I stayed with him, at his pace, which was fast enough. I broke away as soon as the spectators came into view.

No one was surprised that I won. I was a member of Rage; I was bound to finish first. Shep congratulated me ten minutes after the race, which pissed me off. Doc winked at me, which made me smile. I don't know what I was expecting, maybe a pat on the back from Blade, a well done from the other members, but instead I got nothing. Even so, I was on a high for the rest of the evening.

***

The second time Shep hit me, I was given flowers, grovelling apologies and promises it wouldn't happen again. I stupidly forgave him, and for a while, things were good between us until it happened again. I know I could have walked out any time, but I loved Shep. At least, I thought I did. And then there was Rage. I didn't want to leave the club. I was making good money from street racing. And I thought that if we'd broke up, I'd be kicked out, so I put up with his abuse. I was too afraid of his temper and strength to hit back when he was stoned. But when he made the mistake of lashing out when he was sober, he got a bloody nose in return.

Shep was in the living room watching TV while I was upstairs getting ready for a night at the Jester. Shep had been unusually quiet since he got home from work, so I was tiptoeing around him, afraid to say or do something that would start him off. I finished doing my makeup and hair and then dressed in tight black jeans and a black halter-neck top. It was chilly that night, and as usual, we were taking Shep's bike. I took a woollen black cardigan from the wardrobe and put it on. I was planning to take it off and stuff it under the seat before we went inside the pub, but it was freezing outside and there was no way I was getting on a bike without it.

"Don't think you're leaving the house dressed like that." Shep snapped at me.

I looked down at what I was wearing. "What's wrong with it?" I asked.

Road Rage

"Your hair looks like you've just gotten out of bed. You haven't got enough makeup on, and your clothes look like you bought them at a jumble sale."

"I wished I looked this good when I get out of bed," I answered.

"Don't you fucking answer me back."

Shep's hand lashed out, the back of it slapping my face. I fell against the couch. He left the house, slamming the door behind him. I sat on the carpet and cried.

I took pride in my appearance; I never went out of the house without a full face of makeup. But when I was wearing the Rage Jacket, Shep wanted me to stand out. I was his and he wanted everyone to know that. I didn't see it for what it was. It was the only time he was openly affectionate with me. He practically ignored me when we were with Rage, so I took what I could get and was grateful for it.

I'd had enough of him and his abuse. I waited until my shaking calmed, and the bleeding in my mouth stopped, then I reached for the phone. Dawn was the only person I wanted to call.

When Shep came home that evening, all his stuff was waiting for him outside. I said what I wanted to say to him through a locked closed door. Luckily, Shep's only door key was still on the kitchen table.

***

It was a late, cold Friday evening. I'd just left the Jester, via the back, and was walking over toward my bike when I recognised Blade's voice. He was having a heated argument with another man. I moved closer, in the hope of hearing what they were arguing about. I didn't recognise the guy who swung the first punch. Blade ducked and punched the guy in the stomach before being lifted off the ground with a left hook. I swung around to see if there was anyone about that could help, or at least keep an eye on Blade, but Rage was still inside drinking. When I turned back, the guy was standing over Blade with a knife. Instinct kicked in and I ran over without a second thought.

The guy raised the knife ready to strike when I lifted my left foot and kicked him in the face. We'd been racing that night, and I was still wearing my thick boots with a reinforced toe. Blood splattered from the guy's face, and I swear I saw a tooth fly out of his mouth. With my hand stretched out, I bent down to help Blade up, but experience had taught me to always be alert. I turned my head and saw the knife coming at me. Managing to duck, I then swung a flat hand to the guy's throat. I elbowed him in the ribs, pried the knife from his hand and, without thought, drove the blade into his stomach. I watched the guy stumble away. I let him go. I'd done enough damage.

"You okay?" I asked Blade.

"Where the hell did you learn to fight like that?" he asked breathlessly.

"Where do you think? Come on, let's get you back inside."

Although I didn't need anyone's help, it soon arrived when I walked back in holding Blade up.

When asked what happened. Blade just said, "Gem saved my life."

I made sure he was looked after and then left the bar before my face turned any redder from embarrassment. Shep acted indifferent about the incident, as though what I did was no big deal.

I hoped that attitude within the club would be easier after helping Blade out. But the difference surprised me.

"Hey, Gem, how you doing?" one rider called out.

"Had a good day?" another asked.

These people had never said two words to me and now it was as though I was their best friend. I did my best to act natural, but I was taken aback.

Blade called me over to his table. I sat and had a drink with him while the rest of the officers acted as though we'd been friends forever. The conversation was natural, and for the first time, I felt comfortable talking with them.

Road Rage

I left it until closing time before finally saying something. I couldn't let it rest. They weren't getting away with treating me like shit for all those months.

"You guys have shown me no respect or offered a hand in friendship. And now because I did what any one of you would do, I'm suddenly regarded."

Blade looked down at his feet.

"It's because we're scared of you," Turbo joked.

Pat joined in. "Yeah, wouldn't want to get on your bad side, now we know what you're capable of. You're a woman for fuck's sake, and Blade said you fought like a man."

I stood up from the table and looked at each of them in turn. "Fuck, if I knew that stabbing a man was all I had to do to get respect, I would have done it weeks ago."

I walked out and ignored the shouts to come back. I heard the pub door open again as I approached my bike.

"Gem, wait a sec."

I turned and faced Blade.

"Listen, I never got to thank you."

"It's okay," I retorted. "I didn't think it was in your nature to show gratitude."

He nodded his head. "I deserve that. I'm sorry about the way we've all – I've treated you. It was wrong."

"What it was, was uncomfortable," I said. "I've had to put up with Shep's abuse and then his childish jealousy and you've never made me feel welcome or wanted. Doc's the only one who's made an effort."

"That shouldn't surprise you," he said. "You know he's got a thing for you." Blade quickly changed the subject. "Speaking of Shep. You let me know if he lays a hand on you again, I'll sort him out."

"Thanks, but he won't be getting the chance. We broke up. It's over."

"It's about time," Blade said.

I looked down at the ground and kicked the dust with my foot.

"Do you think they'll be a problem with us both being in Rage?" I asked.

"I doubt it. But if it came to it, Shep would be out before you."

I looked up at him in surprise.

"His temper is unpredictable I don't need junkies in my club. He's lost control. I think he loves speed more than his bike. If that boy is not careful, he's going to fall and far."

"Are you serious about keeping me in?"

"Hell yeah. You're a better racer than Shep anyway."

"Thanks, Blade. That means a lot."

"Goodnight, Gem," he called as he started to walk toward the pub.

"Goodnight," I called back.

***

I was mentally exhausted with all the emotions I'd been through in the last few days. I felt relieved that the club had finally accepted me and relief that Shep was out of my life for good. Well, out of my personal life; I wasn't sure how I was going to feel about seeing him most nights. I wasn't certain if we could be friends, as our break-up wasn't pretty. There was no way I was walking away from Rage now. Shep would just have to suck it up.

Luckily, he kept his distance from me. Even so, there was a stormy atmosphere when we were together. The others did their best to lighten the mood.

At ten thirty that following Friday night, I was sitting on the starting line along with Jimbo and Suki, my two competitors. The officers of Rage were standing to the left of me, silently giving me their support. It was a clear, starry night. Perfect conditions for a race.

The flag went down, and I got a good start off the line. However, I was halfway down the straight, going flat out, when I saw red flags being waved from the side lines. It was the signal that none of us wanted to see. Cops had

Road Rage

been tipped off. I watched my competitors break off and speed away up different roads. Spectators were running in all directions. I slowly squeezed the breaks and then skidded to a stop. Before I had time to decide which way I should go, I heard the sirens in the distance. Turning the bike around, I accelerated down the road. I saw the flashing lights in my mirror. The cops caught sight of my bike and started their pursuit.

I couldn't shake them. Every turn left me alone on the street, and before I could take a breath of relief, the cop car would come screeching around the corner. I was as familiar with the roads as they were, so no one had an advantage.

My heart was thumping and sweat ran down my face. I was scared that with the speed I was going, one false move could have me off my bike and seriously hurt. But that didn't stop me dodging traffic. I knew that if the cops caught me now, I'd have the book thrown at me. That's why I drifted recklessly around corners and traffic lights became a blur. The cops couldn't get my address from the DLV; thankfully, I was riding an unregistered motorcycle.

Another car soon joined the pursuit. I needed to get the bike off the street. I knew it was only a matter of time until a police helicopter would be flying overhead.

The only way I could lose them would be by cutting down the nearing alley and then going over the fields. The cops wouldn't be able to follow me down the alley, but I knew they'd be using a GPS and would try to corner me off. I thought ahead. There were four possible routes they could take to get to me, and, with only two cop cars, I knew I had a good chance. Once through the alley, I could get to Blade's house quickly.

They couldn't follow me across the fields, as the nearest entrance from the alley was a public footpath, just big enough to allow my bike to pass. By the time they took the long way around, I was long gone.

I didn't allow myself any hope until I spun up Blade's

gravelled drive and stored the bike safely in the garage. Removing my helmet, I took off my sweat-soaked jacket and then collapsed to the ground. My legs were like jelly, and I couldn't stand, even if I wanted to. Shuffling across the cold concrete floor, I pulled myself up, leaned against the wall, and tried to control my frantic panting. Blade found me there, still breathing heavily.

"We wondered what happened to you," he said.

"I have to get the bike off the streets. It's too recognisable now," I said, not bothering to turn my head. Every part of my body was stiff and achy.

"No problem. I'll take care of it," Blade answered. "You look as though you could do with a drink."

"You're not far wrong," I answered and took his outstretched hand. He pulled me off the floor, reached down to pick up my jacket and then followed me through into the lounge.

I replayed the chase to him as I sipped a brandy, allowing the alcohol to warm my throat. I was still exhausted, and my body shook from adrenaline.

"You've had a long night," he said. "Take a shower and then you can use one of the spare rooms. I don't think you should be riding anywhere tonight."

"Thanks, Blade. Shit, what am I gonna race with now?" I cursed. "How do you guys afford three or more bikes?"

Blade smiled. "Don't worry about that. Rage will sort you out. You'd better get some sleep; you look exhausted."

"Yeah, I will. Cheers."

"Night, Gem."

"Night," I said, giving him a hug. He smiled but looked uncomfortable.

I took a long shower. The flow of water massaged my aching body. I could have easily stayed there all night, but I was too darn tired. I found a baggy t-shirt in one of the drawers of the bedside cabinet. I put it on then climbed under the snug duvet.

The sound of tapping on the bedroom door woke me up. Sitting up, I called out.

Road Rage

Doc's head appeared around the corner. "You decent?" he asked.

"Yeah," I answered, and rubbed the sleep from my eyes. "What time is it?"

"Blade said to wake you around twelve. See if you want breakfast."

I threw the covers off and saw Doc's eyes quickly avert. I reached for my leather trousers.

"Heard you had a thrilling time last night?"

"You could say that."

"From what I hear, you were lucky in more ways than one."

I shrugged and zipped up my trousers.

"Did everyone else get away okay?" I asked.

"Yeah."

"Good."

He was looking my way again, so I reached down and pulled off the t-shirt. I smiled when I noticed his head was turned.

He waited until I was dressed before he spoke again.

"Blade's out, but he said to help yourself to anything in the kitchen. My Yamaha's in the garage for you and you're to race with Blade's Ducati."

I stared at Doc. "Are you serious?"

"Well, yeah. You don't think we're gonna let a patched member of Rage ride around on a 250, do ya? And you have to ride the circuit again. What did you think you were going to use?" He laughed. "Come on, I've just put some coffee on for ya."

"What are you going race with?" I asked.

"No worries, I'll use the Ninja."

I should have guessed he would have more than one bike at home.

Resting his arm over my shoulder, he steered me out of the room.

I made scrambled eggs on toast for both of us. We chatted throughout and continued after taking our coffee into the lounge.

"What are you doing here anyhow?" I asked him.

"Blade asked me to come over and babysit."

I scowled at him.

"Okay, maybe baby, was the wrong word. I guess he thought you could do with some company."

"And he called you?"

"Yeah." he nodded. "You're not disappointed, are you?"

I smiled. "Not in the least. I couldn't wish for better company."

We stared at each other. I couldn't take my eyes off his face.

I knew it was a mistake to go out with a pretty guy like Shep. I'd always been attracted to big guys, you know, the kind you can cuddle onto. Doc wasn't just bearish; he was one of the nicest genuine blokes I'd ever met.

I could see something happening between us. Others saw it before I did. For instance, Blade calling Doc over to the house. Okay, he knew we were friends, but maybe he saw something else. It was so easy to talk to Doc and feel comfortable, not worry about putting my foot in my mouth like I sometimes did. He made me happy. Didn't I deserve some happiness? I'd turned over a new leaf, and I was ready to live the life I deserved.

As I listened to Doc talking, I thought about all the wrong decisions I'd made, and how my life used to be. My teens were rebellious, which then landed me in the arms of the Hawks. At the time, I was thrilled to be associated with the name and I did everything I was told and took what they dished out. That included getting set up in fights, taking hard drugs and being a Hawk's plaything whenever they wanted. Looking back, I can't believe I allowed myself to be used and abused like that. I thought that was what I wanted and what I deserved. I didn't know any different.

"Gem," Doc called, waking me from my thoughts. "You okay? I lost you for a minute."

"Sorry. Yeah, I'm fine. My mind just wandered. Tell me, how did you get involved with Rage?"

Road Rage

"I was racing the circuits. Blade approached me and asked if I had a sponsor and then he invited me to join the club. I didn't know about the side-line until after."

"Yeah," I nodded. "I was just thinking about that. How the public sees official MCs and what really goes on behind closed doors. I guess I thought Rage was different."

"It's a different world, isn't it?"

"Yes, it is."

I wanted to change the subject. "Umm, do you think Blade will mind if I take the Ducati out for a spin before I race? I want to get a feel for the bike."

"I think that's what he'd expect." He stood up. "Why don't we go for a ride now? No time like the present."

"Great idea," I answered.

Blade's Ducati was in pristine condition; in fact, it looked as though it had never been ridden. It was a beauty, and although he would have killed me for christening the bike Lady, the shiny red and black paint work reminded me of a ladybird. She had some kick to her. I found her a lot harder to control than my Suzuki – definitely a man's bike.

***

Two days passed when I got a call from Blade

"West has called you out. You're racing tonight. Be at the pub by nine."

This is what the club had been waiting for. My race against West was gonna bring in some big bucks, and I wasn't about to lose. I had a name, street cred, and a reputation as a winner, and now West wanted a piece of me. I'd know how much Blade put on me when I got my ten percent, I thought hungrily. I wanted this. I could already taste the victory.

I met up with Blade in the bar and he pulled me to one side.

"You've won four out of four races," he said. "Now I want you to lose."

I stared at him. "You want me to lose?" I repeated.

"Yes."

"How much you putting on this race?" I asked.

"Enough. Listen, this is between us, understand?"

"Yes and no," I answered.

"Don't make it look too easy. I don't want Rage accused of fixing the race. It's got to be a close call. Here's five hundred," he whispered and put a roll of money in my fist. No one saw the exchange. "And you still get your ten percent, okay?"

"Okay," I said.

I didn't know where Blade was going with this. I wanted to keep up my winning record, but he was the president and, as a member of Rage, I had to follow his orders.

Although there were other members racing that night, mine was the one everyone was talking about, and would continue talking about after I lost the race. I was not looking forward to it, especially as everyone was rooting for me, and I was about to let them all down, apart from Blade. Five hundred pounds. Five hundred pounds, I kept repeating in my head.

There were loads of spectators already waiting when we got to the rendezvous point. Word must have gotten out.

West was sitting on his Ducati with a big grin on his face and two blondes standing either side of him. I wished I could wipe that smile off his face, but I knew he'd be shouting about his win for weeks, months even. I turned my sight back to the bike in front and followed the convoy through the deluge of spectators.

I was first up. It was such an anticipated race that no one was willing to wait or interested in watching other racers. I saw a lot of money exchange hands as I suited up. Sitting on my bike, waiting for the flag to drop, my heart was racing. Adrenaline was pumping, but this time it wasn't because of the coming rush. Inside, I was furious. I could take West. There would be no contest.

While I was trying to get into the 'zone', I pictured another race with West; this time, I won, and as I had lost

Road Rage

the last, the stakes had been raised. I pictured myself with a helmet full of notes. A thought occurred. Blade was a smart man; maybe this was just the beginning of the hustle.

As soon as the flag dropped, my bike flew. I was already in the lead, and, from my mirror, I saw West closing the gap. The blur of spectators quickly passed, and then it was just me and the road ahead. I allowed him to come alongside of me. It was best if it looked like a dead heat. Man, I was so close, I could taste the victory. I needed to ease off slowly, but my body had other ideas. My grip was frozen.

I could see the finish line. My heart was pounding. My breath stuck in my chest. I finally managed to move my fingers, and that's when West's front tyre overtook mine and crossed the line first.

I slammed on the brakes and skidded to a stop.

"Fuck, fuck!" I yelled, banging my fists on the tank. I wanted to throw my bike down in disgust, but it wasn't her fault. Instead, I rode over to the side and parked the bike before taking my helmet off and throwing it on the ground. For good measure, I kicked it across the road. Anyone in the vicinity could hear my verbal abuse. They kept their distance. It was obvious I was upset, but not for the reason they thought.

Blade found me leaning against a wall, my arms crossed tightly against my chest.

"I know that must have been hard," he said.

"You've no fucking idea," I spat, and then walked away from him.

Doc then came jogging over. "What happened, Gem?"

"He had a better bike," I said.

"Did he?"

I saw the look in his eyes. He knew the truth.

"Come on," he said, nudging my shoulder. "I'm racing next, and I need your support."

I smiled. He didn't need me. He had enough support.

However, I stood at the starting line to watch him and even put a small bet on him. I knew he'd win for me. Out of elation, I ran up to him and planted a hard kiss on his lips. Doc pulled me to him. His mouth opened, and we kissed fervently. I had never felt anything like it. It was literally electric. The hairs on my arms stood up, and I swear I saw a spark. I loved the taste of him, and I wanted more. I had never felt so much passion from one kiss. Whistles from our audience broke our special moment. We stepped away but couldn't take our eyes off one another.

"Whoa!" I spoke.

"My sentiment exactly," Doc replied breathlessly.

"About bloody time," Blade shouted.

I don't know about Doc, but I had a huge grin on my face and was red from embarrassment.

"Come back to my place," Doc whispered. I nodded my head and boy, did my heart race.

I knew what was expected from me from Shep. I had to behave like a slut, take it every which way and act as though I enjoyed it. I did enjoy the sex part, but behaving as I did in the bedroom, like I was a Hawk's whore again, just bought back shameful memories. I didn't want to go that route with Doc. He knew little of my past, but I assumed he'd expect me to be experienced when it came to sex. I just didn't want to take the lead on this one.

We walked into the house but had barely got through the door when we started kissing. It was just the same, the passion that flowed through me was so intense. His urgency also grew, and although I'd decided I was going to follow Doc's lead, I didn't want frantic sex.

"Slow down, hun," I whispered. "I'm not going anywhere. We have all the time in the world."

"You're right, sorry," he said, backing away. "It's just I've wanted you for so long. I've been fantasising about having you, and I worried that this was just a dream, that I'd wake up in my bed alone, then cleaning up after another wet dream."

Road Rage

"You dream about me?" I adjusted my clothing and smiled at him.

"All the time."

"Let's make this dream a reality." Taking his hand, I led him upstairs.

Doc certainly took his time. I couldn't go on anymore I was burning up with desire.

"Now, please," I begged.

Hours passed as we made love, but it wasn't all perfect. Doc's a heavy guy, so we couldn't do missionary position without risking my suffocation, and he's big. I mean enormous. When he took me from behind it hurt- but in a good way. I refused to spend the night. I wanted to take things slow with this relationship and not make any more mistakes.

Doc rode back to my apartment with me. We made out beside the bikes and then he watched me walk into my block.

I didn't know Shep had put a lot of money on me to win the race. He'd been lying in wait. I didn't know until he kicked in my front door and attacked me.

"You fucking bitch," he screamed.

I ran up the stairs, but he grabbed my ankles and pulled me back down almost knocking me out. He dragged me off the floor and then threw me against the wall. I could tell from his angered strength that he'd been using again. Something told me it would be the last time he'd beat me.

"You know how much fucking money I lost because of you? You shit!"

He swung his fist and punched me in the face.

"Don't," I cried out.

He blocked my escape as I ran for the front door.

"You did it on purpose. You lost deliberately. I saw you ease off."

He hit me again and then threw me to the floor.

"Shep, it wasn't my fault," I pleaded.

I couldn't tell him the truth. He didn't give me time to explain.

Sitting on my chest, he pinned my arms under his knees and then reached into his back pocket and pulled out a knife.

My eyes widened in fear when I saw the blade.

"No, don't do this. I'll get you your money. Please, Shep don't hurt me," I begged.

His hand covered my muffled scream as the knife sliced the corner of my left eye straight down to my jaw. He did it slowly, as though he had all the time in the world. He wanted me to feel the pain.

The blade sliced through my flesh like a burning flame. I felt him push the knife deeper as the muscles in my face tore apart. He gripped my chin so I couldn't move. Silent tears dripped down my face and mixed with the pouring, warm blood. I felt weak and was glad I wouldn't stay conscious for much longer.

My vision just started to fade when I felt Shep being lifted off me.

I forced my eyes to stay open as I watched Doc throw him out of the front door.

"Stay with me, Gem," Doc called out before my eyes closed.

When my eyes flickered open again, Doc was staring down at me, his face etched in concern.

"Gem, you're okay," he assured me.

I didn't feel okay. The left side of my face was throbbing. The pain made me want to vomit. I looked around anxiously, but my fear lessened when I realised I was in the hospital.

"Don't worry, the club's gonna put some hurt on Shep," he said.

"Where is he now?" I worried.

"Locked up. Someone called the police." He looked down at the white, starched bed sheets, refusing to meet my eyes.

"I'm not pressing charges," I said adamantly.

His head whipped up. "Why the hell not?"

I reached for his hand. "For two reasons. Firstly, I will

never stand in court and testify against another brother, even after what he did."

Doc raised his eyebrows.

"That's my own code of ethics," I explained.

"And what's the second reason?"

"What's stopping Shep from informing on the club, cutting a deal with the cops, by telling them about our races?"

"I see what you mean. I never thought about it like that. I guess it was a stupid thing to do."

I squeezed his hand. "No, it wasn't, Doc. It was sweet, and I understand why you did it. Thank you."

He bent down, leaned in close, and gently kissed my lips. I didn't resist.

When he broke away, I tried to smile, but the left side of my face was tight and couldn't move the muscles. I waited until the pain subsided before talking.

"I'll contact the station in the morning and drop the charges. Let him stew for a while."

Doc nodded.

I had to ask. "What will you do to him?"

"We'll take away his colours. He's out of the club for good. Don't worry about the rest."

Without any warning, tears started to run down my face.

"Gem. What's wrong? That shit deserves everything he gets."

I shook my head.

"Are you in pain?" He asked anxiously.

"No," I sobbed. "Doc how can I go out in public looking like this?"

"Don't talk like that. It doesn't make a difference to me how you look. You'll always be beautiful to me."

He ran his finger down the old scar on the right side of my face.

"It's not the first time you've been knifed, is it?"

"Guess I have a set now," I cried.

"You can hardly see the old one now. Look, let this

wound heal and if need be, I know a few plastic surgeons." He smiled.

I was feeling pretty low, and it didn't matter what Doc said to reassure and try to cheer me. Nothing was gonna stop me from feeling sorry for myself.

I left the hospital and went home to find the door fixed and the house tidied. I couldn't see a speck of blood anywhere. Although the floral air-freshener they'd used was trying to disguise it, the odour of iron still hung in the air.

I couldn't get the image of what happened out of my head. My home didn't feel safe anymore. Doc invited me to stay with him, but I thought it was too soon, so I took a room at Dawn's house. I didn't even have to pack. Rage did it for me.

I was angry. Furious with myself and the world, and I took it out on my bike. I pushed her to the limit, opened her up on every opportunity. I won every event, but my radical racing didn't go unnoticed by the club. I needed the speed, the thrill of danger and, with every race, I wanted to push it further. I was dangerously out of control. However, I needed to vent my anger. My looks were ruined. I know it's a vain thing to think, but my looks gave me confidence and after what I'd been through with the Hawks, I needed all the confidence I could get.

Doc never once commented on how I looked, but I knew what he was secretly thinking. I tried hiding the fresh scar by letting my hair fall forward but that wasn't enough, so I walked around with my head low, afraid to give eye contact to anyone. I knew what I looked like, what everyone was thinking. That's why Shep did it, to ruin me. He knew that slicing the other side of my face would cause more hurt to me than a gun shot. He knew me too well.

***

"You can't beat him," Blade told me one Sunday evening.

"Wanna bet?" I replied and put my helmet on to drown out the rest of his objections. I was determined to be faster no matter what it took. A reckless action that I was about to pay for.

I'm not sure how the accident happened. I think I swerved to miss something in the road; maybe it was a cat. I remember feeling the back wheel beginning to spin, and then I was sliding. There was nothing I could do to stop the inevitable. The bike slid away from me. It went one way. I went the other. I'm not sure how far I tumbled, twisted and rolled. I just let gravity take me. When I finally came to a stop, I lay on the ground, and took short, wheezy breaths. I didn't want to think about what I'd done to Blade's bike.

I heard feet running up the road toward me and then Doc started yelling my name. I wished he would shut up. My head was killing me. I was lying on my belly, my arms and legs splayed out on the ground.

"Gem, can you hear me?"

Doc laid on the ground beside me, his head level with my face.

"Doc," I whispered. My voice was hoarse and sounded funny.

"Fuck! You scared the shit out of me," he said, as he removed one of my gloves and gently took hold of my wrist.

"Sorry."

"An ambulance is on its way."

"No," I tried to shout, but it came out as a shriek.

"It's okay. Everyone is taking off. Get the hell out of here!" He shouted to the riders and spectators who wanted a closer look.

I heard the running of feet and then engines roaring away.

Doc rummaged through his bag and then shined a light into my eyes.

"Is she okay?" I heard Blade ask.

"Gem, can you move?" Turbo called.

"Get them out of here, Doc," I whispered. "Lie if you have to."

"You guys better take off; cops may turn up any minute. I'll stay. She's gonna be fine. I'll call you at the hospital," he said, as he laid his jacket over me.

"Sure. Call me as soon as you hear something."

I heard the bikes roar away.

"It's just you and me now. How bad are you hurt?" Doc asked.

Tears started to run down my cheek and soak into the sponge of the helmet. At least I hoped it was water and not blood that was wetting my cheek.

"I can't move. I've been trying to move my legs and arms, but I can't."

I started sobbing. I couldn't control it.

"It's okay, babe. Don't get upset. I'll fix you up. Don't you worry about that."

"What if I'm paralysed?"

Doc took my hand and squeezed.

"Can you feel that?"

"Yes."

"Good. Try to move your fingers for me."

My thoughts and energy ran down my arm, into my hand and through the tips of my fingers. I felt a tingling sensation.

"Good."

"Did they move?" I asked.

"Yes, Gem," he quietly laughed. "Stop worrying. You're gonna be fine."

"How's my ride?" I asked, and then yawned.

"Gem." His voice sounded distant, as though he was floating away.

What a time to be tired, I thought, as my eyes closed, and I slept.

I woke up as a nurse was taking my blood pressure. She asked me a few routine questions like did I know where I was and what happened. I only had to look down at the state of me to know I'd come off my bike. My left arm was in plaster, and my right knee was bandaged tightly and resting on what looked like a hammock. I could feel my ribs had been taped as I had problems catching my breath. I felt sick, but thankfully pain free.

Doc came in to check up on me. I was so glad to see him and to receive a warming smile. He checked me over; being a total professional until the nurse left. Sitting on the edge of my bed, he pulled me to him. He held me for a while and then laid me back against the pillow.

"When I saw you come off, I thought I'd lost you."

"I'm sorry."

"Promise you'll never do anything like that again. I think I aged overnight."

I smiled. "Pinkie promise," I said and lifted up my little finger.

"How do you feel?" he asked and then started kissing me all over my face. Little gentle butterfly kisses. When his lips met mine, we kissed deeply, and I allowed the passion to wash over me.

"Better now," I said after I got my breath back.

I loved him. More than anyone I loved before. His kisses took my breath away, leaving me wanting more. I felt safe with him, and he made me laugh. He made me feel special. Even while lying broken in bed, I was bursting with happiness.

"Meds should be wearing off soon, so I'll give you some more morphine. Do you feel sick at all?"

"Yeah, a little."

"Okay, I can give you something for that as well."

"So, what's the prognosis, Doc? Give it to me straight."

I thought I was ready for the truth.

"You're fucking lucky to be alive. I knew this was going to happen sooner or later the way you've been racing, pushing yourself. Well, it's gonna be a fucking long time until you ride a bike again. Your left arm is broken, and you've cracked three ribs but that's the least of your problems. Your kneecap is shattered. There were bone splinters everywhere, it was a mess to clean up. You've got another three ops to go on it, and you'll be off your feet for at least six months, maybe longer."

"Shit. What am I going to do?" I cried. "I need to race, and I have to work. How am I going to pay my rent?"

"You're so fucking materialistic!"

My mouth closed shut. He'd never spoken to me like that before.

"You should be glad you're alive, not worrying about the fucking rent. You could have quite easily broken your back and been in a wheelchair for the rest of your life. Think about that, why don't ya?"

"I'm sorry." I wiped away the tear that was rolling down my cheek.

Doc shook his head and then held me in his arms.

"No, I'm sorry, I shouldn't have said that. You've been through enough without me upsetting you as well. Look, don't worry about the future. I'll take care of everything. I'll take care of you. I promise. Now try to sleep. You need plenty of rest if you're gonna recover fully from this. You've got a long way to go, Gem, but I'm here to help you."

I was in the hospital for nearly three weeks while I recovered from the knee operations. I had regular visits from Rage, and Doc saw me as often as he could, dividing his time between the hospital and club duties.

I was dreading going home. I had no idea how I was going to cope on my own. Even using two crutches, I couldn't walk well. And my arm being in plaster didn't help. I looked like a fucking walking mummy. It was my fault I was in this mess, and I knew it was a matter of having to get on with things and cope.

Only I didn't go back to my apartment. In fact, I never stepped foot in the place again. Doc took me straight from the hospital to his place.

"I can't ask you to do this," I said as he helped me out of the ambulance.

"Then don't ask," he replied.

Doc had organised his house so that I could get around

Road Rage

in a wheelchair. He put special handles in the bathroom, so I could get on and off the toilet seat without having to ask for help. He came up with the perfect solution. I thought it was a temporary arrangement just until I got back on my feet.

I was lying on the bed, my leg resting on a hammock attached to a winch. I couldn't find anything decent to watch on TV, so I was zapping yet again when I heard the doorbell ring. Doc was downstairs making sandwiches. I heard the door open, quiet mumbling, and then Doc came into the room.

"You feel like a visitor?"

"Sure," I said, assuming it was a member of Rage as I'd had no other visitors since I'd been laid up for the last two weeks.

"Who is it?" I asked.

"A colleague from One Stop."

"You're kidding." It only took a second to guess who it could be. "Grey hair and glasses?"

"Yeah, friend or foe?"

"Foe, I think. I don't have any friends there. Send her up. This will be interesting."

It had to be Joyce, my supervisor, sent to check up on me by the dickhead manager.

"Oh, my lord," she gasped when she saw me. "Oh, Gemma what happened to you?"

My left arm was still in plaster, so I lifted my right hand and gave a small wave.

"Car came out in front of my bike; there was nothing I could do."

She nodded her head and sat down on the chair beside the bed. I watched her eyes go from my arm, down my leg, and then to the wheelchair at the far corner of the room. Tears started to well in her eyes. Removing her glasses, she wiped her tears before saying, "My Sam is talking about getting a motorbike."

"How old is he?" I asked, assuming Sam was a boy.

"Sixteen. Listen, Gemma, would it be cheeky of me if I ask to take a photo of you. Maybe if I show it to him, it will put him off the idea."

Yeah, I thought, also proof for the dickhead down the road.

"Sure."

I tried to look pitiful for her as she took the picture with her mobile phone.

"Joyce, you know if Sam really wants to ride a motorbike, you can't stop him."

"I know." She bowed her head.

I continued. "This was just a freak accident. You're more likely to get run over by a car than come off a bike. And statistics show there are more car crashes than bikes."

"I suppose so," she said. "But they are so dangerous, just look at you. You could have been killed."

I thought back to the incident and my weeks of hospital hell.

"Yes, I could have, but I wasn't and as soon as I get back on my feet, I'll be back on my bike again."

Her expression was one of shock.

Doc then came into the room. "Can I get you anything to drink?" he asked.

"No thank you. I can't stay." She smiled back at him.

"Gem, you need any more meds?"

"No, I'm fine for now," I answered.

Joyce waited until he left before speaking again. "So, you really are living with your doctor."

I nodded.

"There were rumours, but one never knows what to believe."

"I was with Doc before the accident," I declared.

'I see." She stood up. "Well, I'd better get going. I bought you a plant. The doctor has it downstairs."

"Thanks. That was nice of you, and thanks for coming."

"Umm, your last doctor's note said you'd be off for another three weeks."

Road Rage

"Maybe longer," I replied.

"Umm, yes. I can see that. Well, take care, Gemma, and if you need anything you only have to call, although it looks as though you have all the help you need," she said with a wink.

"I have a nurse who takes care of me when Doc's at work." And racing with Rage, but I didn't mention that part.

She patted my hand gently before leaving the room.

A day later, I received a bouquet of flowers accompanied by a card all signed by One Stop.

It wasn't until I was finally able to hobble around the house that I found my possessions stored in boxes. My clothes and personal effects were on display as if I'd been living there for years.

My worst fear had come true. I'd lost my home and was dependent on a man.

When Shep had asked me to move in with him, I'd said no. It wasn't that I didn't want to live in a house which boasted three bedrooms, a parlour, huge kitchen and two bathrooms, not excluding the acres of land that surrounded the property. My problem was I didn't want to give up my place. It was my home. Although small, it was comfortable, and I was surrounded by memories and things I loved. I was worried that if the worst happened, and we separated, I'd be left with nothing.

This time, I wasn't worried about that 'what if.' I'd already considered Doc to be an ideal lifetime partner. I couldn't see myself with anyone else. So, what if I had to depend on him for a while? I'd make it up to him once I'd recovered. I vowed to be the best patient and girlfriend the man had ever had.

The pain was excruciating, the boredom worse. I'd learnt my lesson. I wasn't going to stop racing. That was who I was. It was part of me. I just swore I'd never be so reckless again. Life was too short.

***

I had a hard day at work and was looking forward to chilling out with Doc. But when I got home, he was waiting for me. Dressed in a blue suit with a cream shirt and holding a bouquet, he stopped me in my tracks. It was hard to forget it was Valentine's Day, what with the amount of chocolates and wine we sold at the store today. But I never thought Doc was the romantic type.

"Happy Valentine's," he said with a smile that warmed my heart.

Dropping my bag, I ran into his embrace.

"Your bath is ready, and I've bought you a gift. It's on the bed."

My stomach dropped. The only thing I bought Doc was a giant cookie in the shape of a heart with the words 'You're my everything' written in icing. I'll do better next year, I vowed.

I was eager to see what he bought me. He followed me inside the room, his smile never leaving his face. Lying on the bed was a red, off-the-shoulder silk dress. It wasn't the usual thing I'd wear to go out. In fact, if you checked my wardrobe, you'd be lucky to find clothing that wasn't black.

"How did you get the right size," I laughed as I held the light fabric against me.

"Hey, I'm not just a pretty face you know," he laughed.

"Yeah, I'm beginning to see that," I answered.

"So where are we going?" I asked as I stepped into the warm rose-fragrant water.

"It's a surprise," he said.

I sat in the tub as Doc gently sponged my back. "Why don't you join me," I cooed.

"The bath is not big enough for the two of us, as well you know," he laughed.

I thought back to the time we first tried to bathe together, and we nearly flooded the bathroom.

"This time is for you. Just relax," he said, then he stood up and left.

Road Rage

I laid back into the bubbles and closed my eyes. I was lucky to have found Doc, well, Doc to have found me. His chocolate-coloured eyes darkened when he was angry; his lips were small and soft, and his cheeks chubby like him. He looked like a cuddly teddy bear that I could adore. I was deeply in love with him. I sighed contentedly.

We went to a five-star restaurant called The Orchid. The food was superb; gourmet style portions but with eight courses it was enough to satisfy. The exotic, rich tastes complemented the crisp white wine Doc chose. The evening was perfect, and I expected Doc to get down on one knee and propose. Although I'd never seen myself as a wife, if he had asked, I doubt I'd have refused.

That night we made love, and it was almost flawless apart from the sudden ache I got. I cried out without meaning to. Doc immediately got off me.

"What's wrong," he asked, his face full of concern.

"Sorry, nothing. I'm fine, just a twinge." I pointed to the bottom of my stomach.

Doc gently stroked the scar that covered the left side of my gut.

"How did that happen?"

"The usual," I shrugged. "A knife fight. I got it the same time as this." I pointed to the scar on the right side of my face.

"You don't believe in playing rough, do you?" he said.

"It was an even fight. She got as good as she gave."

"You want to talk about it?"

"No. That was my past. Just now and again I get reminded," I said as I rubbed the scar on my stomach.

"It looks as though it was a deep wound."

"Yeah, the bitch tried to slice me open." I bit my lip after the words spilled out.

"Why do you hide behind a soft manner?" he asked.

"It's not who I am anymore," I replied.

"You're wrong," he said and then looking down at the scar, he said quietly, "Scars like this never heal."

I wondered if he was referring to the physical or mental scars.

*****

"Where's Gbh?" I asked as we sat in Blade's living room drinking beer.

"Haven't you heard," Pat sniggered. "He got pulled in last night for drunk and disorderly conduct."

"No," I gasped. "What happened?"

"Same ole," Doc said. "Had one too many and got into a fight. At the Jester."

"Over a woman, no doubt," Turbo interrupted.

"Smitty told him to take the trouble outside, so Gbh throws the guy out the fucking window and then turns and says, 'There, trouble's out.'"

I couldn't help but smile as I pictured the scene.

"Yeah, well it wasn't the first and won't be the last," Blade said. "Our lawyer is sorting it out. He should be back tomorrow."

"Have you ever been inside?" Doc asked me.

"Not a stint in prison no, but I got arrested once -- mistaken identity."

Blade raised his eyebrows. "On to business," he said, thankfully changing the subject.

That night, when I was back home with Doc, I asked him if he'd ever been arrested.

He shifted in the chair. "Yeah, once or twice – drug related." He picked up the newspaper and started to read.

"And?" I pressed.

"I was in a dark place." He refused to elaborate and switched the TV on.

But I could relate. I knew the dark place he was referring to, dependent on a substance that was slowly soaking up your will to live. The voice of reason faded away until there was nothing left but a dark, endless hole.

*****

Road Rage

I thanked God that I wasn't going down a steep hill when I squeezed my brakes, as nothing happened.

I panicked. It didn't matter how many times I squeezed or how much pressure I put on the lever. Nothing was going to make the bike slow down. It didn't stop me from trying, though.

Luckily, I was riding on a road I knew well. The bad news was there was a tight corner coming up fast. I was already doing seventy-five and speeding up. For now, I had to control the bike. I knew the road was going to level out after the curve, but I honestly didn't think I could make the bend going as fast as I was.

I had a choice. I could give it a shot and either end up going off the road and probably seriously injure myself, as I had no idea how steep the drop was. Or, somehow, I could miraculously make the curve in one piece. The only other option I had was to deliberately slide off and hope that I didn't total myself and my ride in the process.

The bend was fast approaching, and I decided to go with the latter choice.

I looked in my mirror and saw the road behind me was empty. I prayed that the road ahead would stay clear both sides.

As I leaned the bike over to the left, my knee scraped. I could feel the leather burning. And the skin of my knee scraping off. I gritted my teeth and tried to block the pain from my head. The plastic was breaking away from the bottom of the bike. I knew it wasn't going to make this trip in one piece.

Reluctantly, I let go of the handlebars and the bike slid away from me while my bum and hips bumped on the road and swung me against a rocky hillside. I watched with sorrow as the bike disappeared off the side of the road and down a grassed embankment. I'd been holding my breath, and I finally breathed, and it hurt.

I wasn't badly injured, but my bum, hip, and right knee

were hurting me. I pushed myself off the ground and managed to limp over to a curve in the road to get away from any oncoming traffic.

I took my helmet off then reached into my jacket pocket and with a shaking hand, took out my mobile phone.

"I crashed your bike," I told Doc.

"You okay?" he asked.

"Yeah, just banged up a little. I don't think your ride was so lucky. It's gone over the side of a road. I'm on the Rushmore straight."

"Don't move. I'm on my way."

I sat on the grass and lit up a joint while I waited for Doc.

How was I going to afford a new bike? I owed Doc big time. Not forgetting I now had to ride around on my 250, which wasn't a good look for a member of Rage. I threw the butt into the road, frustrated with myself for crashing Doc's bike. What happened? Where did I go wrong? Questions raced through my mind as I replayed the incident. I was still going over things when I saw Doc racing down the road toward me.

He skidded to a stop as I stood up. Taking off his helmet, he rushed over to me.

"You, okay? Are you hurt?" he panted.

"I'm fine. Doc. I'm really sorry about your bike. I don't know how long it's gonna take me, but I'm gonna pay you back, I promise."

"Don't worry about that. My insurance will cover it. What happened, Gem?" He hugged me and I shivered into his jacket.

"The brakes failed. I couldn't stop," I said.

"Shit. You could have been killed." He held me tighter. "Come on, let's get you home."

"What about the bike?" I asked.

"I'll come down later with the guys and pick it up. Stop worrying about the damn bike, will ya?"

I looked up at him and smiled.

Road Rage

My shivering didn't stop as we rode back to the house. In fact, it got worse. I guess Doc could feel my body shivering. He probably could hear the chattering of my teeth over the roar of the engine. I knew it was the shock. And no matter how hard I tried, I couldn't calm myself down. My body wouldn't listen.

I sat on the sofa with a glass of Jack Daniels in my hand, sipping the bourbon slowly while I struggled to hear Doc talking on the phone in the next room.

"Yeah, she's okay. Fucking lucky she wasn't killed – I don't know. I haven't had a chance to look. Gem seems to think it's totalled. – Yeah, that would be cool, cheers. I don't want to leave her on her own. Okay. Hey, Turbo, check something for me, will ya? Gem said the brakes failed, only I had it serviced two weeks ago. I'll fucking kill Henry if he's skimming on me. - Yeah, something like that. Okay, cheers mate. Yeah, I'll tell her. Bye."

"Who was that?" I asked when he came back into the room.

"Turbo and Gbh are picking up the bike. They send their love."

"You can go with them. You don't have to babysit me, you know. I'm fine," I said defensively.

"You'd think I'd leave you alone after what you've been through? Now, shut up and drink your JD, so I can get you another one."

He smiled as he watched me down the bourbon.

Later that evening, Doc got a telephone call. This time, he didn't leave the room.

"I thought as much." Doc grabbed my hand and squeezed it. "I'll be down tomorrow morn to check it out myself. Yeah, I have a few ideas."

Doc closed the phone and then sat beside me on the sofa. His serious expression gave me concern.

"Who have you pissed off lately?" he asked. "Think hard, Gem."

"Umm… no one I can think of. Why?"

"What about that guy you beat last week? He was pretty pissed off, wasn't he?"

"Who, Jacob? Nah, he was cool. We had a drink after the race. Don't you remember? Doc, what's going on?"

"It wasn't a mere accident. Mechanical failure. Someone had messed with your bike. Turbo said the brake pipe had been cut."

"What!" I jumped up. "Are you sure about this?"

Doc stood up and put his hand on my arm. "Yeah, there was brake fluid running down the side of the bike."

"Shit, you're serious."

"Someone tampered with your bike, Gem, and wanted you hurt, and I think I know who."

I tried to picture who hated me enough to want to seriously hurt or even kill me.

"Shep," I whispered.

Doc nodded his head. "Wouldn't be the first time he's tried to kill you."

My hand instinctively went to my cheek and touched the evidence of Shep's previous attack.

"It's okay. I'm not gonna let him get away with this. I promise. You're my lady now and no one will touch you again. Leave Rage to sort this out."

I was too stunned to answer. I couldn't believe that Shep would mess with my brakes. I knew the guy didn't like me, but I didn't think he'd go that far.

I didn't ask what happened to Shep, but I never saw him again. I hoped he took the easy way out and skipped town.

I'd trashed so many bikes that I wouldn't take Rage up on the offer of another bike, so I bought a second-hand Honda Fireblade. It was in perfect condition and the guy I bought it from was happy enough to take installments.

***

It was a gorgeous, sunny morning, the perfect time to give the bikes a good wash. I was outside on the drive listening to a rock station on the radio when my favourite song came on. I danced to the music while soaping Doc's bike.

Road Rage

I was enjoying myself until Gbh turned up on his Suzuki. I ignored him and continued with my task. It wasn't as if he was there to see me.

"Hey," he yelled. "You can do mine when you're finished."

"Sure," I answered as I scrubbed the sponge along Doc's wheel spokes. "Just leave fifty quid on the tank."

He walked up the soapy, wet drive and stood beside me.

"So how long until you total this one?" he mocked

I threw the sponge in the bucket of water and then stood up.

"What's that supposed to mean?"

"Well, what's this one – number three?" He sniggered. "You've gone through more bikes than anyone I know. Maybe it's about time you learned to ride."

"Now just a minute..." I moved close to him, ready to spar if he wanted, but he continued.

"I've had my baby since I joined the club, and no one rides her but me."

I so wanted to say I wouldn't be seen dead on that piece of junk, but that would have been childish, especially as Gbh's Suzuki looked in pristine condition.

"Doc's inside," I said. "And make sure you wipe your fucking feet."

Gbh laughed before going through the garage and entering the house.

"Shit head," I muttered. I was angry because he was right. I'd wrecked two bikes in the few months I'd been a member, and I was too damn poor to be able to afford another one. I hated Gbh for reminding me of that fact.

I had a big race ahead that night. Jake was known as a winner. He raced for a club called Stripes. There were sixteen stripes on Jake's jacket, each one representing a win. I felt I had a chance of winning the race; after all, I was riding Blade's Aprilia. Nevertheless, I was on edge most of the day. My mind was somewhere else other than work, which didn't go unnoticed by the manager.

Sitting up straight with my hands on my lap, I looked

into my manager's face.

"After what you've been through, I have cut you some slack," he said. "Even kept your job open for you. But lately, I've had numerous complaints from customers and staff."

"I'm sorry, Mr. Smith. I really appreciate all you've done for me." Go fuck yourself, you oily twat! "I promise I'll do better."

He put down the pen he was twiddling and then shuffled some papers on his desk.

"Yes, well, okay. It's the first time you've been sent to the office, so we'll just call this your first and last warning."

Yes, Sir and would you like me to bend over your desk so you can spank me with a ruler? "Thank you, Mr, Smith. I won't let you down."

I was earning good money from the club, and Doc seemed to think it should have been my number one priority. He couldn't understand why I was still working at the supermarket. I couldn't tell him it was because the job was keeping me straight. Without it, the club would have taken over my life, and I couldn't allow that to happen again.

After I won the race against Jake, I was called out by many contenders. But I was now in the position to pick and choose who and when I raced. I decided to let my contenders stew for a while.

I was doing well on the circuit also. I felt proud to sit under the Rage tent, this time welcomed and wanted. I was known around the circuit and was treated with the same regard as the rest of Rage. Respect! Boy, did it feel good. Now in the intermediates, I could really open my baby up, and boy, did I feel the need for speed. I've never felt more alive than when I was racing.

***

I was dressed in my racing gear even though I wasn't racing. Blade wanted his riders ready, as you never knew when you'd be called out at the meets. I was sitting on my bike sipping a beer and chatting to Dawn and Pat when

76

Road Rage

Blade came strolling up and took the bottle from my hand.

"That's enough. You're racing tonight," he said.

"Who?" I asked.

"One of the Aces. Clive, you know him?"

"Seen him once or twice," I answered.

Ace had a good rep almost as good as ours. They always caused a stir when they showed up unexpectedly at the meets. The guys were young posers that liked to show off their bikes, but they were also known as winners.

"Hey, hold up a sec," Gbh called out. "I'm up to race Clive next."

"Leave it," Turbo warned.

"What is the bullshit?" Gbh demanded.

Blade turned to face him. "I want Gem to take him on. Ace has put on a bet that I'm not about to turn down."

"Fuck that!" Gbh yelled. "I've been waiting a long bloody time to race this tosser. I'm not fucking stepping down."

I didn't give a shit whether I raced Clive or not, but I was pleased to see how upset Gbh was.

"What's going on?" Bre asked as she joined us.

"Blade's giving my race to Scar Face."

I jumped off my bike and charged at Gbh the same time Doc, who had just come around the corner, ran at him.

Turbo grabbed hold of my jacket, and I struggled to get out of it so I could tear the motherfucker's eyes out.

"You son of a bitch," I yelled.

Doc laid into Gbh with relentless punches. I'd never seen that anger from him before.

"Leave it, Doc," I shouted, still in the grips of Turbo. "I don't need you to fight my fucking battles."

A crowd had started to gather, eager to see the fight. Gbh was taking his jealousy of me out on Doc. Both fought as though they wanted to kill each other.

Pat stepped forward.

"Leave them," Blade instructed. "They need to blow off some steam."

I couldn't stay and watch, especially as Blade wouldn't allow me to punch some sense into them.

"Okay, get off me," I yelled to Turbo.

He released his grip and I walked away from the scene.

"Wait up," Bre yelled. "What was that all about?"

"Doc was defending her honour," Dawn answered as they walked beside me.

I stopped. "I don't need anyone defending my honour," I argued. "I can take care of myself."

"We know," Dawn said, "but that's what the men do when someone insults their lady."

"Doc shouldn't have got involved. I could have taken that shithead." I walked away.

"Leave her," I heard Bre tell Dawn.

I needed to calm down. I still had the race ahead, and I needed to focus and stay sharp. Blade had already pushed his Aprilia to the starting line by the time Pat found me and told me they were waiting. Clive was sitting on his bike casually chatting to another club member. The ace card on the back of their jacket displayed to everyone that they thought of themselves as being top of the deck. His friend nodded my way then left. Clive did up his jacket and was putting on his gloves when I approached. He didn't greet me, but I decided to speak to him anyway.

"So how come we don't see your MC down here much?"

"Got better things to do," he answered, and then put his helmet on.

Arrogant bastard, I thought. Not only did he think he was the best. He also thought he was too good to associate with Rage. The guy needed to be taught a lesson on how to respect his elders, I decided.

Forest Road was one of the easiest to race. Marshals were standing at the top of the lengthy road, ready to radio in when the lights changed to red, stopping any traffic that might have been on the road at two thirty in the morning. There were no bends on this course. It was a straight road, and the faster rider crossed the finish line

Road Rage

first. We were both sitting on an Aprilia. So far, we had the same odds. It all depended on who was daring enough to go flat out; reaching around hundred and twenty M.P.H before having to brake sharply prior to crossing the lights. I knew what I was willing to risk to win. I only hoped Clive wasn't feeling so brave.

Doc was standing at the starting line watching me. He'd have a black eye by tomorrow, I thought, as I studied his bruised and battered face. I knew he wanted to talk to me, clear the air. I assumed Blade ordered him not to approach. I searched around and spotted Gbh standing alone. His arms were folded, giving attitude.

"Motherfucker," I whispered under my helmet.

I took a deep breath, faced the front and concentrated on the race.

Thankfully, I got off to a good start. It was a close call, but I won by just a small margin. I knew my win would keep Rage happy for the night, but I wasn't ready to celebrate yet. I had unfinished business to attend to.

My moment came when we returned to Blade's house to continue the party. I'd been watching Gbh closely. I followed him upstairs and saw him enter the master bathroom. Making sure the coast was clear I reached into my back pocket and pulled out my switch blade. I waited until I heard him pissing, then I walked in. Standing behind him, I raised my arm and held the knife to his throat. The flow of urine stopped.

"Now you listen good, you pathetic little..." I looked over his shoulder, "Yes, little man. You ever insult me like that in public again, I swear I will slit you open. You have no idea what I'm capable of, do you? I don't need Doc to fight my battles. Do you understand me? Nod your head."

I moved the blade an inch away from his neck. Once he confirmed he understood, I dropped my stance and stood back. Gbh zipped up and turned around. His face was pale. He looked shaken. I was glad I'd gotten to him. I still had the knife in my hand, but I stood casually.

"I've let your childish jealousy slide, but now it's starting to affect the club, and I can't have that. So, what is it? You jealous that I'm a better rider than you, is that it? If I lose a few and get you back on top, will that make you feel superior?"

Gbh never said a word, just stood staring.

"Sorry, but I'm not going anywhere..." The door to the bathroom opened and a woman stood outside surveying the scene.

"Piss off," I told her. She turned back around and left quickly.

"I like winning," I continued, "and no one, especially a pathetic twat like you, is gonna make me feel bad. We need to make things right between us." I folded my knife and put it back in my pocket.

Gbh held his arm out "I'm sorry, Gem. I should never have said that about you. I was just mad, and it came out."

I didn't care to hear his apology. I knew we'd never be friends, but I didn't want there to be problems with him and the others, especially if it was over me.

"Why don't you go back down and apologise to Blade and Doc, and then we can forget this ever happened?"

"Yeah, okay," he said.

"Good."

I opened the door and left him inside. I pitted the fluffy beige towels that were about to have Gbh's grubby hands all over them.

Leaning against the hall wall, I sighed deeply, smiled and then went downstairs to face the others.

***

Man, I used to love going to bikers' rallies. That was one part of being a Hawk that I really enjoyed. It's a time to meet up with old friends, drink, kick back and hang loose. So, when Tex suggested we visit Matlock for their annual festival, I could not wait. It had been years since I'd been

Road Rage

in such a large gathering and now, as a member of a respected MC like Rage, I wondered how different it would feel.

As a Hawk, I demanded respect and God help any woman or man that didn't give it to me. Because of the size of our numbers, we owned the festivals. No matter which other clubs were present, we were the kings, given respect through fear. Rage was known around the country because of their riding skill and their position on the circuit. I wondered what kind of reception we would receive.

We left town early but were in no hurry to get to the festival, so we made plenty of stops on the way. There's nothing better than the honour you feel when speeding down the motorway in formation. You know that everyone is staring, envious of your bike and the club, wondering where you're off to and wishing they could join. We stopped off at a small village. The pub had a lovely lock running near it and we sat in the sunshine drinking cold beer and just soaking up the atmosphere.

We finally made it to Matlock by one o'clock. The festival was a place to put bikes on show, and ours would certainly get attention. But no one wanted to stay behind and keep an eye on them, so we parked down from the field where the rally was being held and then walked up. My excitement grew as we got closer to the noise. The smell of the vendor vans woke my appetite, and my mouth watered at the thought of a greasy burger with fried onions smothered in tomato sauce. As we entered the festival, I pointed out the nearest burger van and then we stood around while orders were given to Blade and Bre, and then we patiently waited for our food.

I stood with the rest of them and surveyed the scene. Music stalls, clothing, food vendors, and, of course, bike memorabilia stalls lined up both sides of the yellow, sun-dried field. And in the middle and at the sides of the booths, people milled around.

I'd just taken the first bite of my burger when I saw them.

Three Hawks were standing in front of a Harley Davidson stall. The golden wings on the back of their jackets were unmistakable. Immediately, I turned my back to them and swallowed what was in my mouth. My hands started to shake and sweat dripped down my neck. My heart raced and I knew I had to get away before I lost it in front of everyone.

"Blade, sorry, I have to go," I said to him and held up my mobile phone. "Family emergency."

"Yeah, sure," he answered and reached out for my arm. "Is there anything we can do?"

I shook my head.

"I'll come back with you?" Doc announced.

"No, Dawn can ride back with Gem. I want you here, Doc," Blade said.

I wasn't about to argue with Blade. I had to get away before my legs buckled underneath me.

Doc looked disheartened and hugged me tight before letting me go. Dawn shrugged then walked into Pat's embrace. He kissed the top of her head. They watched us walk away.

"Call me when you get home," Doc called.

I turned my head and smiled.

"Dawn, I'm so sorry about all this." And I really meant it. I knew how much she was looking forward to the rally.

"There's always next year," she said and shrugged.

"I'm glad you're here, though, I could do with some company." I couldn't imagine riding all the way back on my own.

I started up the bike and Dawn hugged onto my back as we rode out of Matlock.

My mind was somewhere else until she nudged my back and got my attention by pointing to a motorway stop. Suddenly, I needed a strong coffee. We got our drinks and sat down at a table. I sipped my scalding coffee slowly as

Road Rage

I stared out of the large window, which surrounded the empty cafe.

"Your phone never rang," Dawn said.

Her statement startled me, and I swallowed the mouthful of coffee, burning my throat in the process.

"You never got a call. You lied. Why? There is no family emergency is there?"

I put my coffee cup down and folded my arms. "Very astute, aren't you?"

"What's going on, Gem? You can tell me. I promise I won't say anything to the others."

"And that includes Doc?"

She nodded. "Of course."

"I saw someone at the rally who I didn't want to see."

"And?" she said. "That's why you left?"

"Yes."

She shook her head. "There's more though, isn't there?"

"It's complicated."

"It was the Hawks, wasn't it?"

I stared hard at her, then picked up my coffee cup and gazed out of the window again. "So, you know about that then?"

"Yeah, Pat told me."

"Great, remind me never to reveal anything else to them."

"I saw the look on your face when you saw them."

"You see too much," I said.

"You should face your fears, you know. Rage wouldn't have let anything happen to you."

I laughed and then turned towards her. "Fear? Is that what you think it was? I'm not scared of those motherfuckers."

Dawn raised her eyebrows.

"Sorry. No, it was just a shock seeing them again after all this time. I should have known they would've been there. Yes, I could have stayed and dodged a couple of Hawks but there are never only two."

I needed to explain it better, try to get her to understand where I was coming from.

"I haven't seen a Hawk for nearly two years. I guess when I saw the patches, all the shit I'd been through came rushing back at me. It was a reaction I couldn't control. It won't happen again."

"Until next time," she said and then sipped her drink.

"I'm not scared about meeting a Hawk," I told her. "I just don't like being reminded of my past."

"You can't keep running, Gem." Leaning across the table she took my hand and squeezed it reassuringly.

"I'm not running anymore," I said.

"Will you tell me something? Be honest," she asked.

"Sure."

"Why did you join Rage? After everything you'd been through with the Hawks, why subject yourself to that again?"

I smiled. "I missed it. Not the violence and drugs. I missed the company. I need to feel as though I belonged somewhere, to feel I'm worth more than I am."

She nodded her head. "I think I get it. Look, I know you have difficulty opening up, so thanks for sharing."

I sighed deeply. "It's good to finally talk to someone about things. Thanks for being here. You're a good friend. Umm, do you think anyone else noticed my reaction?"

"Nah, they are not as astute as me."

We laughed, finished our drinks and then got back on the bike and rode home.

***

I never thought I'd be attending a funeral on my birthday, but here I was, dressed in black, a pack of tissues in my pocket, as I slowly followed the procession of bikes.

A week before, we had gone for a run to Blackpool to celebrate the New Year as a club. And boy, did we celebrate. Most of us were drunk twenty-four seven, and that's where the stupidity came in.

We were all staying in the same hotel, the Golden Sands. It was a pretty decent place. Food was good but there was no night-time entertainment unless you count the old guy banging out sing-along tunes on an un-tuned piano. God knows what the old folk staying there thought of us, seventeen patched members not including partners, lounging at the bar, dressed in our leathers and jeans.

That Friday evening, we had one drink in the hotel bar and left for the town. January in the UK can get pretty cold, but we were padded up well, and the brandy helped to warm our bones.

Most of us were over the limit by the time we left the third bar, but as we were experienced riders and knew how to handle our bikes, we took it steady.

Blade was looking for a bar that would be willing to shut the doors and allow after-hours drinking.

I don't know if he was showing off, but I saw Tex ride out of formation. The next thing I heard was an almighty crash, metal on metal. Pat, who had seen the accident, said Tex did a wheelie straight into a garbage skip. The bulb on the warning lamp wasn't working, and he didn't see it. I was surprised Tex could see anything that night after what he drank.

There was nothing we could do to save him. Doc pronounced Tex dead on the scene. I didn't dare go over and look at the wreckage. Blade spent most of the early morning signing papers and arranging for the body to be transported home. The rest of us went back to our hotel rooms and raided the mini bar to drown our sorrows.

I'd never met Tex's parents. Not once had they been to one of our club's BBQ. Doc lost his parents in a fatal car crash three years ago. I lost mine to cancer. I just assumed as Tex never mentioned them, that they were already dead.

It was a very sad day for us all, and from the slap Blade received across his face as he gave his condolences, it was obvious Tex's parents held Rage responsible for their son's death. Because of this, we didn't think it was right to go to the wake, so we held our own at the Jester. Blade ordered take-out. So, while loud rock music was played, we munched on pizza, drank beer and said farewell to our friend.

***

"Tazz is coming home," Blade announced to everyone in the bar that evening. The place erupted in cheers, and bottles were raised.

"When is he flying in?" Gbh asked.

"Tuesday and we'll have a welcome home party on Wednesday evening, if that's okay with you, Smitty?" Blade asked the landlord.

"Hell, yeah," Smitty answered as he poured a pint.

"Let the good times roll," Turbo hollowed.

"About bloody time," Bre said.

It was obvious by the excitement of the others that Tazz was well known and respected.

"Who's Tazz?" I asked no one in particular.

"Tasmanian devil," Turbo laughed. "He's Australian."

"He's the founder of Rage. The king of the streets," Pat added.

"But I thought you started the club," I said to Blade.

"No. I just take the reins when Tazz is away."

"He's in the armed forces," Doc said. "Been serving our country for the last fourteen months."

As long as I've been here, I thought.

"Where's he stationed?" I asked.

"Iraq."

"Shit. I bet he's seen some action," I said.

"Yeah, but don't ask him about it when you meet up. He likes to leave the battle behind when he comes home," Blade informed me.

I listened quietly for the rest of the night as Rage talked non-stop about Tazz. I was intrigued and excited to meet the legend.

When I finally got home, I asked Doc what Tazz was like.

Road Rage

"He's as straight as they come," he replied. "Takes no shit and he's smart."

"Smarter than you?" I joked.

"He's cool, Gem. You'll get on fine, don't worry."

I shrugged as though it didn't bother me, but I was worried. I wanted Tazz to like me. It was important that he accepted me as the others had done. I was determined to make a good first impression. But something was bothering me, and I didn't want to talk to Doc about a possible conflict, so I confided with Bre.

"Man, I've missed that guy so much," she said after I brought Tazz up in conversation.

"You two close then?"

"You could say we've been through the wars together, not literally," she laughed.

I swallowed bile before asking, "And Shep, were they good friends?"

Her silence confirmed my suspicions.

"When they were together there was no separating them. He's gonna take it hard." She grabbed my hand and suddenly sat up with a jolly face. "Don't fret, Tazz knows what Shep was like. Once he hears what went on, I'm sure he'll understand."

I shook my head "I doubt that. He knew Shep was a bastard, and yet they were still good friends. He's gonna love me," I said sarcastically.

Bre just shrugged and reached for her coffee mug. The subject never came up again.

Wednesday night came and I was as nervous as hell. I tried on at least four different outfits settling for black jeans and a silver sparkly top. Doc laughed at my anxiousness, but that didn't stop him adding to my dread by saying, "He's gonna be checking you out, and he's bound to wanna see you ride."

"Why, your opinion not good enough for him?"

"He takes the club very seriously," he told me sternly.

"How long is he back for?" I asked.

"Dunno. I haven't spoken to him yet. Blade will take a back seat now. Tazz will take over the presidency."

I didn't want to dislike the guy before I met him, but my feelings were leaning towards that way. It didn't seem right for Blade to have to step down for a guy who turned up now and again to race. In my opinion, Blade ran the club well and Tazz hadn't got a clue what had been happening.

Smitty went all out for Tazz's homecoming. British flags flew proudly outside the pub and inside, the bar was full of red, white and blue. A huge banner took up the top of the bar; the black bold print read THE HERO RETURNS. To the locals, he was a hero for serving their country. He wasn't just a hero to the club; he was a legend.

Tazz stood among the sea of familiar faces. He was a tall man, thin but muscular. He wore his blonde hair shaven short. Round glasses perched on the end of his small nose.

"Welcome home, man," Doc greeted him with a hug and a manly pat on the back.

"Good to see you Doc. How you keeping?" Tazz looked straight at my face. Although I was used to people staring at my scars it still made me uncomfortable.

"This is Gem, latest recruit and my lady," Doc announced.

"Hey, Gem. Nice to meet you." Tazz held his hand out and we shook.

"Good to see you're finally settling down." He patted Doc on the back and smiled at me.

"Tazz," a woman's voice screamed. Then Bre came running over and jumped into his open arms.

"It's good to see you, honey," he said, and kissed her on the cheek.

"How long are you here for?" she asked eagerly.

"Four tours are long enough for this boy," he answered. "I think I'm home to stay."

"Yes," Bre yelled and hugged him again. "I see you met Gem. She saved Blade's life, you know."

Tazz turned his head. His eyebrows were raised, and he looked at me questionably.

"Slight exaggeration," I said, hoping I wasn't blushing.

"Bullshit," Bre laughed. "She's an asset, Tazz, and you should see her ride."

I smiled and then turned my head to hide my embarrassment.

"I'll look forward to it," Tazz said.

"What's that?" Turbo asked, as he, Pat and Gbh joined us.

"Bre was just telling me what a good rider Gem is. I'd like to see for myself."

"Yeah," Pat jumped in. "You two should go head-to-head. Sorry, Gem, but my money's on Tazz."

I laughed. "Anytime."

"Okay," Tazz answered, "how about Friday night down at Jessie's Lot?"

I knew the place well. "Sure. Why not?"

"Where the hell is Shep?" Tazz bellowed. "It's not like him to miss a good party."

My stomach dropped and I looked to Doc for support.

"Come on," Blade said as he put his arm around Tazz's shoulder and started to steer him away. "You need a refill."

"He's gonna hate me," I said to the others as we watched Blade quietly talking to Tazz in the corner of the bar.

"Yeah, he doesn't look so happy about it," Gbh said.

"But he won't tell him the truth, will he?" I looked at Gbh accusingly. "You know, about what really happened to Shep?"

No one answered. I felt them watching me as I saw Tazz turn my way while Blade continued talking. Pat coughed to gain our attention then he told a crude joke to get us all laughing. Tazz never spoke to me again that evening, but I caught him staring.

I didn't see him or the others again until Doc and I met up with them at Jessie's Lot on Friday night.

He was sitting on a Ducati Multistrada 1200. I'd never seen one before, and it was a beast of a machine. Seated on the monster in orange and black stripe racing leather, he looked a formidable sight, a prince among bikers.

Doc and I parked our bikes with the others and then walked over to where Blade was chatting with Pat and Dawn. This wasn't an official street meet, so only Rage and few from down the pub were present.

I took my gloves off and put them in the helmet then ruffled my hair, eventually giving up with the tangles, I settled for tucking the sides behind my ears.

"How did Tazz take it?" I asked Blade.

"Not well, but he'll come around. You just need to prove yourself even more. Try to beat him if you can."

"Any advice?" I asked the guys.

"He has the same riding style as you," Pat answered. "The only chance you'll have is around Penny's Bend."

That was the name we gave the sharp corner after the straight. It came up fast, bending to the right and then three twists followed. Not only was it the place I had to overtake, but it was also the most dangerous part of the run. The bike needed to lean right over to make the twists in the road. One false move and the tyre could slip, and you could lose control of the bike. I'd seen it happen before. I'd never had a problem with this part of the race, but then again, I was always in front with someone chasing me, not the other way around.

"So, Gem," Tazz said, as I pushed my bike into position. "Let's see if you can live up to the hype."

He put his helmet on before I could reply. I followed suit. Once my gloves were on, I sat on the bike and revved up. Bre threw the flag down, and then we were off.

Tazz went flat out, and I had no problem keeping up with him, but his front tyre was always ahead of mine. I kept turning my head towards him. I couldn't stop watching. His movements were solid, yet flowing, and he gripped the throttle like a vice.

I knew I had to concentrate harder when his back wheel passed me. Tazz was in the ideal position. Now he could watch for when I made a move to pass. Every time I tried,

Road Rage

he moved left or right blocking my path. Penny's Bend was fast approaching; I knew I had only one shot. I eased off a little hoping my ruse would pay off. It did. Tazz made the mistake of slowing as he took the bend. I opened her up and managed to get beside him before he realised what had happened. The bikes were beside each other, our tyres nearly touching. I pulled the bike over to the left, my knee pads skimming the road as I fought for control. I swiftly pulled up and leaned to the right, ready for the next twist. Then I levelled out and opened the throttle the moment I was back on the straight. The quick movement startled Tazz, and he swerved to avoid a collision. My bike stayed in front and was the first to cross the finish line.

The officers of Rage didn't celebrate my win; I guessed they didn't want to rub the loss in their president's face. But I knew from the smiles and the wink I got that my success was acceptable.

Tazz came over to congratulate me. "Good job there."

"Thanks," I said, trying not to let my grin spread the width of my face.

"You've got some skill, girl. But that was a risky move you pulled."

"It worked," I answered curtly.

He nodded his head. "So how are you doing on the circuit?"

"Not bad; always in the top three of Intermediate class."

"Nah." He shook his head. "You should be riding up there with Turbo and Blade."

"What, with the pros?"

"Yeah, you've got skill and stamina. I'd like to see how you get on."

"I'd need a bigger bike," I said, hoping I wasn't pushing it.

"Oh, I'm sure we can sort something out," he answered with a smile. "Come on. I owe you a drink."

Putting his arm around my shoulder, we laughed as we walked over to where the others were waiting.

Only I didn't get my big bike and I never got a chance

to move up a class. Fate played a deadly hand.

In the early hours of Friday morning, Doc's bleeper woke us both up. As was usual when this happened, Doc reached for the phone.

"Doctor Webber here. You paged me," he said.

I listened to the one-sided conversation and my heart started racing. I sat up in bed and waited.

He climbed out of bed the same time he put the phone back on the cradle.

"I've got to go," he said, as he started to dress.

"What's going on?"

"Tazz has been attacked and they need me for surgery."

"Oh, my God. I'm coming with you."

He didn't argue. We had only been in the car for five minutes when Doc's mobile phone rang. Caller ID showed it was Blade.

"Hello," I answered.

"Gem, where's Doc?" Blade asked. He sounded out of breath as though he was running.

"The hospital just paged him. We're on our way. I guess you heard the news then?"

"Yeah," Blade Answered. "Some fucker caved Tazz's head in with a baseball bat."

"Jesus!"

"Let me speak with Doc."

I held the phone to Doc's ear and tried to listen to the conversation. When Blade asked how bad it was, Doc replied, "It's not good, bro."

After we got to the hospital, Doc jumped out of the car and ran inside. I parked the car, locked it up and then waited in the hospital corridor until the others showed up.

We hugged, but the guys wanted answers from me. I told them all I knew was that Tazz was in surgery. I got coffees from the machine then I sat down beside Pat and Turbo. Gbh was at reception filling in forms while Blade paced the corridor.

"Who would do this?" I asked no one in particular.

Road Rage

"Oh, we know who it was," Blade spat. "Smitty called me after it happened."

"The attack had nothing to do with Rage," Turbo growled. "The fucker has no association with the club. He's not even a fucking biker. We barely know the guy"

"This was personal," Pat said. Turbo nodded his head in agreement.

Blade stopped walking and started clicking his knuckles. "Smitty said Tazz was sitting by the bar, finishing off his pint. Apart from Smitty and Suzie, there was only one other customer left. In comes this guy, baseball bat in hand, bold as brass. Walks over to Tazz and whacks him over the head. Tazz never had a chance to defend himself. Smitty said Tazz were on the floor when the guy hit him again. Then the fucker spits on him, throws down the bat, and walks out."

"Jesus Christ." I didn't know what to say. I couldn't imagine anyone hurting Tazz intentionally.

We waited three long hours until Doc found us and gave us the news.

"He's in ICU, critical but stable. We removed a blood clot from his brain."

"But he's going to be okay though, isn't he?" Turbo begged.

"The next hours are crucial. We won't know the extent of the damage until he wakes up."

"If he wakes up," Gbh added, as he walked toward us.

I sat down on the chair, numb. Pat had his hands covering his head when he suddenly jumped up.

"This guy fought for our country," he yelled. "Four fucking tours in Iraq and not a scratch. He's here for what, one week, and he gets his head bashed in; probably be a vegetable for the rest of his life."

"Don't you say that," Blade growled. "Don't you fucking say things like that. Our boy is strong. He's gonna get through this, isn't that right Doc?"

We all looked to Doc for confirmation.

"He's a fighter," Doc answered. "Look, I've got to go. You should take off. There's nothing you can do here. I'll call you if there's any change in his condition."

"I'm staying," Blade said.

"I'll keep you company," I offered.

There was no way I could sleep now. If I went home, I'd just be staring at the walls. At least here I'd have Blade to keep me company and I'd be the first to hear any news.

The white, empty corridors were creeping me out. I was about to go outside and get some needed fresh air when Blade whispered, "He's a dead man, Gem."

Yes, there was going to be retribution. There would be if any of Rage got jumped, but this was different. Tazz was our founder. A hero to the people, and the way the premeditated attack occurred, how vicious and unnecessary it was, called for a quick and just retaliation. We sat in silence, listening to the muffled noise of the hospital waking up.

Tazz never regained consciousness. Hours later, Doc informed us that Tazz had been declared brain dead and that the ventilation he was on was doing the breathing for him.

Physically, and mentally exhausted, the three of us left the hospital around eleven that morning. Blade said he would contact the others, and that we were to meet his at his place at four in the afternoon.

I waited until we got through the front door before talking to Doc.

"I'm so sorry," I said.

Doc walked toward me, and I pulled him to my chest.

"I just wished there was more I could have done," he replied. "You should have seen the mess, Gem. The first blow split his head open; the second mashed his exposed brain in."

I felt sick at the vision.

"Even if he'd woken up, he would have been brain damaged."

I didn't know what to say. All I could do was be there for Doc and stand by any decision made by the club. My gut was telling me that Tazz wouldn't be the only fatality.

Road Rage

The others were already there and waiting when Doc and I arrived. We hugged, but nothing was said. I could tell they were wired though, ready for action. Doc and I were the only ones that sat still. Turbo paced the room; I was going to tell him he was wearing out Blade's carpet, but now wasn't the time for jokes. Gbh kept getting up from his seat and looking out the window. I wondered what was so fascinating out there. And Pat couldn't stop fidgeting. All heads turned towards Blade as he came into the room.

"It's going down tonight. Suzie said the fucker plays pool down at the Cue Club every Friday night. We'll follow him from there, cut him off at the river. It's out of the way. We shouldn't be disturbed. All agreed?"

One by one, the officers of Rage gave their vote. I was surprised my opinion was asked for, especially as I wasn't going to be involved in the ambush.

"Agreed," I said without hesitation.

However, I felt sick to my stomach knowing I'd probably just sentenced a man to death.

Doc left the house early that evening, as he was meeting the boys for a drink before heading down to the Cue Club. He didn't say much before he left; there wasn't much we could say. I told him to be careful and hugged him. He smiled back, but it was tight and forced.

After I watched him ride away, I closed the front door and then threw myself on the couch. I understood how conflicted he must be feeling. He was a doctor. His job was to save lives, but tonight he might be put in a position where he had to take a life.

I tried to eat something, but I felt sick. I couldn't concentrate on the TV, and I couldn't get into the novel I was reading. By nine o'clock, I gave up. Grabbing my jacket, key for my bike and my helmet, I left the house. I didn't want the others to catch me following, so I rode down to the river, parked the bike off the road by the riverbank, then stood and waited.

The hour dragged on and my heart raced with every vehicle or bike that passed by. It was chillingly cold, and fog was starting to build up. I shivered in my jacket, stamped my feet and jogged on the spot to try to keep warm. It had just passed ten thirty when I saw them. The car was in front with two passengers. Rage were close behind. I waited until they passed, and then I jumped on my bike. It took several attempts to get her going. By the time I caught sight of the others, Rage had already stopped the car on the bridge. Blade's and Gbh's bikes had blocked the exit. The other bikes were either side of the car. I slammed on my brakes just as Blade was pulling the guy out of the car. A woman was screaming. The guy was thrown to the floor, and I saw Gbh stamp on the man's head. Then the others rushed in and started booting the guy. A gun shot rang out and I saw Pat drop to the ground. I started up my bike and raced forward, just as the woman jumped out of the car and ran screaming up the road toward the bridge. Doc was helping Pat to sit up when he saw me pass. I didn't stop.

She'd just climbed over the side of the bridge when I skidded my bike to a stop. Throwing my helmet to the ground, I ran over to her.

"Stay where you are," she yelled, as she pointed the gun at me.

I stepped back and held my palms up.

"It's okay. I'm not going to hurt you," I lied. I couldn't wait to get my hands around her throat. However, as I watched the gun shake in her hands, my legs turned to jelly. I could feel my pulse racing through my neck.

"I killed him," she yelled. "He was hurting John, so I shot him."

Now was not the right time to remind her that John had left my club president brain dead.

"It's okay," I said quietly, surprised that my voice wasn't shaking. "He's okay. You didn't kill him."

"They're going to lock me up. I can't go to prison," she cried.

Road Rage

Her body shook as she sobbed loudly. I thought she'd either lose her grip of the gun, or her hold, on the bridge, either way I knew I had to calm her down. I wasn't scared for myself; I was scared of what she might do.

"What's your name?" I asked and took a step forward.

"Karen."

"Give me the gun, Karen. I promise you're not going to get into any trouble. Just give me the gun." I held my hand out hoping she would hand over the weapon, like they do in the movies.

"I shot him. But I had to. They were hurting John," she repeated.

"I understand. Look, why don't you come back over here, Karen, and we can talk for a while."

"They're gonna lock me up. I killed a man. They were hurting John. I had no choice. Oh, God, I can't go to prison."

I was getting frustrated and, unfortunately, I let my anger get the better of me.

"Look, someone was bound to have heard the shot and called the police. They are probably on their way, so we don't have much time. Jesus! Get your arse back over here now."

"I can't go to jail," she sobbed. "Oh, God I killed a man. I shot him."

I knew she was in shock and what I wanted to do was shake her out of it.

The next thing I saw was Karen raising the gun, putting the barrel to the side of her head and squeezing the trigger.

Nothing happened. The gun jammed. I sank to my knees and bowed my head.

"Tell your friend I'm sorry," she said quietly.

"No!" I screamed, as I lifted my head and watched her body fall into darkness.

I ran over to where she'd jumped, but it was too dark to see anything.

"You stupid bitch," I cursed, as I pulled down the zip of

my jacket, threw it on the ground, and then, untying my boots as fast as I could, climbed over the bridge railing and jumped. I didn't have time to think. I did what anyone would have done. But it wasn't about saving her life. It was about saving myself; I knew that if I didn't try, I would spend the rest of my life blaming myself for her death.

The shock from the coldness of the water took my breath away. Before I'd even gone under, I was having problems breathing. I fought my way to the top while my chest tightened. Finally, my head reached the surface. I gulped the freezing air greedily. I knew I had to get out of the water before my body went into shock. My teeth chattered so hard, I thought they would crack. I saw the back of Karen's white blouse billowing in the water. Her hair fanned around her head and her arms floated at her side. I swam over but could barely close my hand as I grabbed hold of her blouse and turned her over. I don't know how I found the strength to swim back to the bank and pull her out. I couldn't feel my hands. My whole body was shaking, but I knew what I had to do. Wasting no time, I started pumping her chest with my closed fist. Pinching her nose so no air could escape, I breathed into her mouth watching her chest rise and hoping it would continue to do so without my help.

"Don't you fucking die on me," I yelled as I continued C.P.R. I stopped for a second to blow warm air onto my hands. I knew I couldn't continue for much longer. My body had a mind of its own. I was shaking uncontrollably. I could barely keep my fist on her chest. My vision was beginning to blur. I was so cold I just couldn't feel anything.

Thankfully, Karen started coughing and the river water gushed out of her mouth. I pushed her over into the recovery position before my strength gave out and I collapsed.

I woke up in my bed, but I wasn't alone. I murmured something unintelligible. I felt an arm squeeze my waist.

"Welcome back," Bre said and kissed my bare shoulder.

I then felt her warm naked skin against mine. It felt

soft. It felt good. I wasn't about to make the effort to turn and address her. My eyes were closed, and I wanted to stay exactly like I was.

"Bet you never thought you'd end up in bed with me, did ya?" She laughed.

"Pat," I croaked.

"He's okay. He got hit in the shoulder. Doc's seeing to him, and then he'll be right over."

"How you feeling?" I recognised the voice immediately. I opened my eyes and saw Blade looking down at me.

"Tired," I whispered.

"You're quite a heroine," Blade chuckled. "That's two lives you've saved. You get some thrill from it?"

I didn't answer. It was a relief to know Karen was okay, but I was too tired to care about anything else. Bre snuggled up closer and I fell into a welcome and contented sleep.

We were all cut up about the loss of our founder, no one more so than Bre. Depression set in and her drinking increased and nothing anyone said or did made a difference. I knew she needed time to grieve, to let it all out, and I hoped I'd be the person she'd confide in. I found her sitting alone at one of the far tables in the Jester.

"Hey, Bre," I said.

She shook herself awake and focused on me with a smile.

"Mind if I join you?"

She pointed to the empty chair.

"How you doing, hon?" I asked.

She shrugged.

I wasn't sure how to bring up the subject of Tazz, so I sat quietly and played with the torn, blue beer mat that was on the table.

"We were like a married couple, you know," she said.

I turned towards her and gave her my full attention.

"There was no separating us," she continued.

"But I thought...."

"No, God no, it wasn't like that. If I was into men, he would have been my ideal partner. We loved each other but there was no sex."

I nodded.

"He made me laugh."

I smiled, "Did you two stay in contact while he was away?"

"All the time. He didn't write very often, though. I still have his letters. He told me he treasured mine, more than letters from his own family."

"You knew him a long time then?" I asked.

"Yeah, way before the club started up. I knew him better than any of them. Maybe that's why it's affected me more." She bent her head and looked down at her feet.

Blade came over and placed two drinks on the table. I casually indicated for him to walk away. He got the message and re-joined the others at the bar.

"We're all grieving for him," I said. "I didn't get to know him very well, but he seemed a really nice bloke."

"He was the best," she said, and then reached for the glass.

"I'll be okay. I just need time. I keep imagining him walking through the door."

We both looked to the pub entrance and then back down at the table.

"I can't believe I'm not going to see him again," she continued. "He was home for good, you know."

I nodded.

"We had so much to catch up on. Plans to make and stuff. But I guess that will never happen now."

I put my arm around her, as she leaned into my chest.

"You're not alone," I told her. "We're all here for you, and if you need to talk anytime, I have a pretty good ear."

"Thanks, Gem."

We continued drinking and I changed the subject, which I thought Bre was glad about.

"How's she doing?" Turbo asked after I left Bre and joined the others by the bar.

Road Rage

"She'll be okay, But, Blade, I don't think it's a good idea if she races for a while. She's not in the right frame of mind."

"No, I wasn't going to," Blade said. "At least not until she curbs her drinking."

"I'll try to spend more time with her," I said. "Try to get her mind off things. Any idea what she likes to do?"

No one answered. Turbo looked down at the floor. Blade looked embarrassed and Doc just shrugged.

"Do any of you know her at all?" I demanded.

"She likes women and fast bikes," Gbh said.

"No shit, Sherlock," I retorted.

"There's an Xtream motor show on, down at Milton Keynes next weekend. I could get you tickets," Turbo suggested.

"Sounds good," I said. "And I'll take her for some retail therapy as well."

"Yeah, we know how you women like to shop." Doc laughed.

"Yeah, but Bre isn't your normal woman, is she?" Gbh said.

All heads turned as we watched Bre pick up her jacket and head for the door.

Tazz's parents didn't want to sell the Multistrada, so they gave it to Blade. Blade said I could keep his, which had been stuck in the garage ever since the crash. She needed a lot of work and money spent on her, but it was still going to be cheaper than buying a new superbike. I'd finished paying off the Fireblade and didn't want to get in debt again.

"I'll ring around and get some quotes," I suggested to Doc as I skimmed the morning newspaper.

"No need," he said. "I'll take the bike down to our usual garage. Henry works on the club's bikes. He's good at his job and you'll get a good deal."

Doc loaded my battered Ducati on the trailer, and then we took her down to the garage.

"Man, you must have been going some to scrape this baby

up," a man in green oil-covered overalls said, as he walked over. "Hey, Doc."

Doc patted him one-handed on the back. "Henry, this is Gem."

"Yeah, I've been expecting you." Henry smiled at me. "I heard about your trouble."

"Can you fix her?" I asked. "Make her look new again."

"I'm sure I can work my magic," he laughed.

"Not a problem," Henry said as he ran his hand along the scratched and buckled tank.

I handed over my key and then followed Doc outside.

"Just a sec," I said and walked back in.

Henry was still standing by the bike looking it over when I stepped up to him.

"I don't suppose you know anyone who could do a paint job?"

"What d'ya have in mind?"

"I'm thinking deep red with large black spots," I answered, hoping he wouldn't think I'd lost the plot.

"Like a ladybird?"

"Yeah, exactly," I cried excitedly.

"I think I know someone who could do that for you." He smiled.

"Thanks, Henry, you're a star."

"What was that all about?" Doc asked when I got in the car.

"Just adding a personal touch," I said.

***

"Hey guys," I greeted. "What's up?"

I sat on Blade's sofa that faced them. This was an official meeting. All the officers were present. I wondered why I was going to get a grilling. What did I do or not do?

"With Tex's death, we now have an open position for an officer of the club. And we think you'd be perfect," Blade said.

"Umm – okay, but what about Bre? She's been here a

lot longer than me."

"Bre's not officer material," Turbo said. "She's cool with it, though."

"And you're more than capable," Pat added.

"Wow. Umm okay. What's the position?"

"With your expertise, we'd thought you'd make a great treasurer. Keep the books so to speak; record outgoings and incoming."

"I can do that," I smiled and looked to Doc. My smile was not returned. His expression unnerved me. He looked worried, nervous even.

Turbo coughed. I turned my head back around to face him.

"You know from Doc how much time is taken up from officer duties. You know how we roll."

I nodded.

"You don't," Gbh growled. "Doc, you tell her."

Doc leaned forward in his chair, his arm resting on the table.

"You're a smart woman, Gem. You see things. You know Rage is not just a racing team."

"Yeah, I had an idea," I said.

I'd heard whispers around the club. Snippets of information and Doc would sometimes disappear days at a time. I never questioned where he was. I knew it was club business, but now it was my business, and I was about to learn the truth.

"So, what is it you guys are into, drugs?"

"No. Guns."

That wasn't what I was expecting. I swallowed the bile that was rising in my throat.

"You're an officer now, so anything you're told stays in this circle," Blade warned.

"You don't need to know the ins and outs of the operation. That's my business," Gbh said.

That was fine by me. I didn't want to know the details of who they sold to and the kind of guns they dealt with.

Gun trafficking! Jesus Christ. What had I gotten myself into? I never thought Doc would get involved with something like that. I knew the club wasn't legit, but I thought it was drugs. There were certainly enough dealings going on inside the club, but guns! I wondered what else I didn't know.

"Now you've had time to digest this information," Blade said, waking me from my thoughts. "Turbo will show you the books and go through our way of doing things. You have to attend every meeting, and your input and opinion will be required."

I nodded.

"There are other perks too," Doc said. "You now get twenty percent on every race you win. You don't pay membership fees anymore and you'll get a nice Christmas bonus." He smiled.

I smiled tightly. I couldn't think about that now. I needed to talk with Doc, alone.

"Congratulations, Gem," Blade said, and stood up with his hand outstretched. "So, who's up for a drink?"

"Sure," I answered.

I didn't get the opportunity to speak to Doc until we got home later that evening.

"Some night," he said as he shrugged off his jacket.

"Yeah," I answered vaguely. I turned and faced him. "How come you never told me? Didn't you think as your girlfriend, I had a right to know what you were involved in?"

"It's not as simple as that, Gem." He put his arm around me, but I shrugged it off.

"I knew you'd act like this," he growled.

"What do you fucking expect? Shit, why do I always put myself in these situations?"

Sitting down on the sofa, I put my head in my hands and sighed. Then I sat up. "I was a member of the Hawks for three years. I know what goes on in an outlaw motorcycle club, but I stupidly thought Rage was different. How involved are you in the operation?"

"I make deliveries and pickups. Don't worry I'm careful."

"It's not you I have to worry about." I lit up a joint and took a deep drag.

"Do you use the same connections?" I asked.

"Mostly," he shrugged. "They're kosher. Nothing's gone wrong yet."

"That's a big yet. It only takes one deal to go wrong."

"Hey, don't worry. We know what we're doing"

"No, you don't," I yelled, and stood up. "I've been involved in this racket before. I know what can happen. I've experienced it first-hand."

Doc stood up. "You've had a rough past, haven't you?"

"Yes. But I was a different person. I knew what I was doing and for the most part, I enjoyed it. No one messed with me. Shep would have found a knife in his stomach if he'd laid a hand on me back then." I paused as a vision flicked through my mind. "But I got out and that wasn't an easy thing to do. I've changed, yet it's still hard to control myself. I don't ever wanna be that person again."

"You don't have to be. You can walk away anytime. No one will think badly of you," Doc said.

"No. I'm in too deep now. Racing is in my blood." I smiled. "Just keep me out of these dealings. I don't want to know. And if you had some sense, you'd do the same."

Doc shrugged. "Like you say, I'm in too deep."

We cuddled up on the couch in silence. I must have fallen asleep as I woke up in bed with Doc lying beside me. I caressed his smooth chest, and he smiled, grabbed me around the waist and pulled me on top of him. We kissed and nibbled each others neck and ears. With passion about to explode, I straddled him and rocked gently until he was deep inside me. I groaned with pleasure as the rhythm increased. He took my breast and sucked it hard while I climaxed. I rode him faster until he came, then we lay in each others arms, naked, sweaty but satisfied.

"I left home when I was sixteen," I said. "I hitchhiked

around the country, living in caravans and waiting tables in roadside cafes."

I don't know what made me start talking about my past. It just seemed the right opportunity, and I wanted Doc to know the truth.

"That's when I met Dekard. The Hawk patch told me I'd get respect if I was with him. We talked, and when I mentioned I was ready to move on again, he asked me to go with him. I didn't hesitate, excited at the thought of a new adventure. I had no idea what I was getting myself into. Those years were a nightmare which I still live every time I close my eyes."

Doc squeezed me tightly. "I'm here, babe," he whispered.

His reassurance gave me the strength to continue. "I liked Dekard. He was good to me, but Trip, the president of the chapter, made it clear he wanted me. Dekard wasn't going to refuse, so I was handed over like a piece of meat. That's when life suddenly got hard. Trip was a sharer, and although I was known as his old' lady, he passed me around the camp, and I didn't dare to complain; many a time I got a fist in my face for saying or doing something Trip didn't like. He demanded respect, especially from his women."

Doc kissed the top of my head. I took a deep breath and continued.

"I could have left then. It would have been easy. I could have, but I didn't. Instead, I stayed and took their shit. I hardened, became a bitch, as was expected from me. I was taking heavy drugs by then just to cope with the violent lifestyle."

"What happened to make you leave?" he asked.

"I was introduced to another female gang, apparently the president of the club used to be a Hawk, and so Trip and she had a history. I took an immediate dislike to them. They were beautiful, slim, polished and young. It made me take a good, hard look at myself. I was an ugly, broken shell and hated the women because of how they made me

Road Rage

feel. They were invited to camp with us and, although Trip warned me not to start anything, I didn't like the way the Hawks respected them. I didn't like the attention Trip was paying to one of the women. Ice was her name, and she was stunning. I was raging with jealously and the female Hawks made it clear they wanted the bitches sorted. It ended in one of the most violent fights I've ever been part of. The women certainly knew how to flight and even faced with numbered odds, they didn't back down. I respect them for that. While I was recuperating in a hospital, I re-evaluated my life, and I knew I had to get out. So, I planned and schemed until I found a way to flee without leaving a trace."

I sat up and took the joint from Doc's fingers. "I moved here, rented an apartment and then started working at the supermarket."

"That must have been hard for you?" Doc said.

I nodded as I exhaled the smoke. "It was hard to adjust to a normal life again. I managed to keep out of trouble by not socialising with anyone. I just kept to myself."

"Must have been lonely," Doc said.

I shrugged. "Gradually, I put the past behind me until I met Shep."

"That part I'm glad about - in a sick way," he quickly added.

I stared at him.

"Well, if you hadn't met that son of a bitch we would never have been introduced."

I smiled and then hugged him while vowing that I'd never talk openly about my past again.

****

Three weeks later, I got the call to go down and collect my bike. I was speechless at the sight of her. She looked better than I imagined she could. I knew the guys would give me some stick about the paint job, but I was ready to take their abuse. I sat on my newly covered leather seat and started her up, and boy, did she growl smoothly. I've never heard her sound so good. We had a meet that night, and I couldn't wait to open her up.

"What the hell have you done to my bike?" Blade exclaimed as we piled out of the Jester to leave for the meet.

Gbh covered his mouth to muffle the laughter.

"Actually," Turbo said, "I think it looks good."

"Yeah," Pat added. "It's certainly gonna get you attention tonight and that's what we need right now."

"Not that kind of attention," Gbh argued.

"Wow," Bre gasped as she stepped out of the Jester. "That's awesome. Who did it?" she asked excitedly.

"Not sure. Henry fixed me up with someone."

"I think it was Chuck, down at Brentel," Doc said.

"Yeah, I've seen his work around. He's talented," Turbo said.

"Man, I've got to get mine done," Bre said, as she stroked the side panels. "It looks wicked."

"Oh, great," Gbh moaned, "and what are you going to get? Fucking butterflies?"

"Hell no," Bre answered. "I want a skull and crossbones."

We laughed and I couldn't keep the smile from my face.

My bike certainly got attention that night and from the reaction it wasn't all bad. Blade caught up with me before we separated.

"You'll never get me sitting on a bike dressed up like that, but it suits you, Gem."

Blade didn't pay compliments very often, so I felt honoured.

"Blade wants to see you," Gbh said.

"What, now?"

"Yeah, why, you too busy to follow an order?"

"No. I'll be there in ten minutes," I said, and then slammed the phone down on him.

Although the sun was blazing, I felt a chill. A shadow covered me, and my apprehension grew, the closer I got to Blade's house.

Gbh was standing outside the door waiting for me. Only two bikes were parked outside. A meeting with just Blade and Gbh; this can't be good, I thought.

"Hey, Gem," Blade greeted, as he offered me a beer. "Take a seat."

He sat on the corner of the coffee table and looked down at me. "I'll get straight to the point. You rode with the Hawks for three years. What can you tell me about them?"

"Everything you've heard is probably true," I answered.

"You don't mess with them. They're an outlaw motorcycle club and have their hands in everything."

As I looked at Gbh then back at Blade. My stomach dropped. "What's all this about?" I asked, already knowing the answer.

"I've set up a deal with the Hawks. They're buying some guns from us. Just a small order to see how it goes."

"How it goes!" I screamed. "They are the last people Rage need to associate with."

"This isn't about Rage," Gbh growled.

"You need your fucking head tested. I'll tell you how it's gonna go down. The idiot that delivers the guns is gonna get his fucking head blown off."

I was pacing the room. Anger was flowing through me, and I wanted to hit someone or something. But I'd kept my anger in check for the last few years, so I stopped pacing, bent my head, and took deep breaths before turning back to Blade.

"You need to get out of this before it's too late," I warned.

"I'm not walking away," Blade told me calmly. "The deal's set up; we're making the drop tomorrow."

"Blade, please don't do this. You've no idea what you're getting into."

I didn't know what to say to him to make him see sense. "Which chapter are you dealing with?"

"The south chapter, a guy named Troy," Gbh answered.

"No!" I yelled. "That's who I ran with. Trip is the president and he's a mean son of a bitch. Trust me, this isn't going to go down well."

Blade moved out of my way as I started pacing again.

I looked at Gbh. "You doing the drop?"

"No," he answered.

"That figures," I sniggered. "So what fool is delivering the guns?"

"Doc is."

"Hell no," I yelled and ran at Gbh.

He gripped my arms before I had a chance to dig my nails into his face.

Road Rage

Blade pulled me away, and then I shrugged him off. There was no way I was allowing Doc to walk among those animals.

"I'll do it," I said without thinking. "They know me. I know how to handle them. I'll make the delivery."

"We need someone who knows a little about guns. Have you ever fired one?" Blade asked.

I sat on the corner of the sofa and was about to answer when Gbh interrupted.

"She ran with the Hawks. I think she knows enough."

I nodded my head.

"Pat will go with you," Blade announced.

"No," I said. "I'm going on my own or the deal's off. I won't put a member of Rage in danger."

"I think you're making a big thing out of this," Blade said.

I didn't answer him.

"What about you," he asked. "If you're so sure this deal is going to go south, why are you taking the risk?"

"They won't hurt me." At least I hope they won't, I thought.

Gbh stood up. "Okay, it's settled. Meet Blade here at five tonight. You'll be taking the van."

Man, I wanted to punch him in his smug face. He'd set up this deal but had no intention of doing the drop himself. Payback is a bitch, I thought smugly.

As Blade saw me out, I laid my hand on his arm. "Keep Doc busy. I don't want him knowing that I'm doing this."

"Yeah, it's probably for the best," he answered.

I had a long drive ahead and needed to sleep, but it wouldn't come. I kept picturing Trip's face, imagining what he'd think when I turned up out of the blue. My mind would not shut off. Blade did as I asked and kept Doc away from the house. I didn't get to see him before I left.

The van was loaded and waiting for me as I pulled up to Blade's house. As I was parking the bike in his garage, he came out and greeted me.

I followed him over to the van, where he then slid the metallic grey doors open and pulled out a black duffel bag.

I wasn't too surprised to see Glocks, Colts and a few Walther semiautomatics inside, but it did make me wonder where and how Blade got hold of AKs.

"I'll call you before and after I make the drop," I said.

"Gem, you sure you don't want someone to go with you?"

"No. I think it's best if I go alone. Just promise me one thing."

He nodded.

"Make this is the first and last time you do business with the Hawks."

"I can't make that promise," he said, showing his authority.

The only way I could get him to understand would be to sit down with him and tell him about my past, only now was not the right time.

"Well, I can promise you this," I said, pointing a finger to his chest. "If you don't, I'll walk away from the club and I'll take Doc with me." I got into the van without another word.

Jeez, riding a motorcycle is so much easier than driving. I was tired, achy and mentally exhausted. And thanks to the one-hour detour I accidentally took, it was pretty late by the time I pulled into the motel. The good thing about the journey was the weather had stayed cool and dry throughout the day.

I left the duffel bag in the van. I hoped it was safe enough. There was no way I was lugging the guns around with me.

The room was basic with sparse furniture, but at least it looked clean and had a TV. I phoned Blade as soon as I was settled. I wasn't supposed to call in, and I think he was surprised I did. The reason I phoned was so I could hear a friendly, familiar voice. I hated being on my own and away from home. No, what I hated was being away from Doc.

I knew that leaving a note wasn't the right thing to do. I should have kissed and cuddled up with him. I'm sure that would have kept me going until he was back in my arms. But instead, I scribbled on a piece of paper that there was a family emergency and that I'd be gone for the night, not to worry and I'd see him tomorrow and explain. The pen kisses were nothing compared to his warm lips on mine.

I showered, changed into my pyjamas, and then climbed under the chilly sheets. Sleep wouldn't come even though my eyes were closed. I finally got out of bed at eight thirty. I'd been watching TV for the last three hours and had enough. My stomach rumbled, informing me it was time for breakfast, only I was so knotted up I didn't think I could eat anything.

The motel I chose was only a few miles from the clubhouse. I was already in Hawk territory. I locked the door and stood outside searching the car park for motorcycles. I saw two Harleys parked outside the roadside cafe next door where I was planning to have breakfast. My stomach dropped. They were the sort of bikes the Hawks rode. Taking a deep breath, I walked slowly towards the cafe.

I saw the bikers before I walked in. They were sitting opposite each other next to the window. Their leathers were on the back of the bench chairs so I couldn't see the patches. I didn't recognise them and that made me relax a little. It would have been stupid to turn and walk away so I went inside and took the furthest table, sitting with my back to them.

The meeting was set for eleven. I stared at the plate of greasy fry up in front of me. The smell of fat and eggs was making my stomach turn. Pushing the plate away, I reached for my coffee. Minutes later, my phone rang. I looked at the caller ID and then switched the phone off. I couldn't talk to Doc now. I knew he was going to get worried, but I wasn't ready to answer his interrogation. I told myself I'd call him after the drop-off.

I could have easily sat there for the rest of the day; my body didn't want to move. Here I was about to do a deal with Trip and to top it off, I was wearing a patch. Trip had no time for other clubs, unless, of course, he was getting something out of it.

I breathed a sigh of relief as I watched the two Hawks leave the cafe. Time was ticking by, and I knew I had to make a move, so I threw money on the table and stood up to put my jacket on. My hands shook as I reached to drain the last of my coffee. Get a grip, I scolded. The last thing I needed was to turn up at their clubhouse, a nervous wreck. I knew that if I was going to get through this, I had to act tough. I had to become a Hawk again.

Driving up the lane, I swallowed the bile when I saw the Hawk's stronghold. The outside was nothing to shout about, just gravel, dirt and dried grass. There were seven bikes parked around the front along with their red pickup truck. Their club house was an old, converted farmhouse. The wall that separated the kitchen and living room had been knocked down, creating a large room which they used as their bar. Upstairs had an office where they kept their files and club funds, a large room where they held their club meetings, a bathroom, and three small bedrooms in case a Hawk needed to crash. Of course, the bedrooms were used for other purposes as well, but I didn't want to think about that.

Shaking away the memories, I whispered, "Let's get this over with," and then climbed out of the van.

Three Hawks were standing outside waiting for my arrival. I recognised two of them. As I climbed out of the van, I saw Besty running back inside. I guess I hadn't changed as much as I hoped. I knew he was letting Trip know about my arrival. I could wait. I wasn't about to do the deal with anyone else anyhow.

I stood with my hands in the pocket of my jeans and glared at the men in front of me.

I heard Trip's laughter before I saw him. He hadn't changed at all. His long ginger hair was tied back, and the tight small plait still hung on the front of his lengthy beard.

It was hard to believe it was nearly three years since I'd seen him. He was still dressed in the same clothes I remembered: a sleeveless jean jacket so he could show off his impressive tattoos and muscles, black plain t-shirt and blue jeans.

"I don't believe it," he laughed. "Ford, well there's a blast from the past." His laughter stopped as he lowered his sunglasses and looked me up and down.

"You look good. You've filled out," he smirked.

"Seeing as you kept me on a diet of speed and pills, I guess I have," I answered.

I thought back to how I looked back in the days of the Hawks. I was bone thin, had short dyed blonde hair and an elfish face caused by my overstretched skin. I looked like death warmed up. Now, I had a healthy glow, meat on my bones, and thick glossy, long brown hair. I could imagine the change he saw. A group of Hawks came piling out of the club to see what was going on.

"Jake," Trip called to a Hawk that stood in line with the rest. "This is Ford. She used to run with us."

"I've heard her name before," he answered.

Trip laughed.

"Best fuck I ever had."

I hoped my face wasn't giving away my embarrassment.

"What about a drink, for old time's sake?" he suggested.

"No, thanks. I don't intend to stay long." There was no way I was accepting a drink from a Hawk unless I wanted to be drugged and raped.

"So, Rage, huh?" Trip said.

I nodded.

"What are you running with those tossers for?" Besty asked.

His black hair was still greasy and long, and he had on his usual Rolling Stones t-shirt. I could tell by the stabbing looks he was throwing my way, we still had unfinished business. He hadn't forgotten.

"I thought you were out of the game for good," Troy added.

"I thought I was," I shrugged. "They're not that different

from you lot."

Besty sniggered.

"So, to business," I announced.

Trip wasn't ready to deal yet. "No one knew where you'd gone. I looked for you, of course." He stared silently.

I sniggered. "You looked for me? You mean you sent your minions out?"

"Same difference," he shrugged. "So apart from hanging with those losers, what else have you been up to, Ford?"

"My name is Gemma," I barked.

"Just because you changed your name it doesn't change who you are," Besty said.

I shook my head.

"It's in your blood," Troy added. "Look at ya. You couldn't stay away from the lifestyle."

I shook my head vigorously, trying to deny what he said. But I knew it was the truth. I was drawn to fast bikes and bad boys.

"This is a one off, as a favour for Rage. You won't be seeing me again. I'm out of the game. I've changed."

"Keep telling yourself that," Besty said.

I was getting angry and upset. "You want to see the merchandise or not? I ain't got time to fuck around."

"So how long have you been with Rage?" Trip continued.

I sighed. "Awhile."

He nodded.

"Look. Let's stop this bullshit. I didn't come here to socialise or reminisce. Are we doing this deal or not?"

"No. I don't think we are," Trip replied sternly.

"Well, in that case, I'm leaving. I have to get back. They'll be waiting for me."

"You're not going anywhere. We've got some catching up to do. Why don't you be a good girl and follow Besty and Troy into the club and I'll join you in a sec?"

"Fuck you," I spat. "I ain't going nowhere except home. You don't own me anymore."

I started to walk back toward the van when I heard Trip

click his fingers. Before I had a chance to run, Besty and Troy were either side of me, gripping my arms.

"Now, now, do as you're told," Besty sang.

"Let me go, you piece of shit," I yelled, as I struggled in their grips. I kicked out at Besty's leg and in return got a fist in my face.

"You need to learn some fucking manners," Trip yelled as the Hawks dragged me, half unconscious, toward the clubhouse. I heard the van door sliding open. Trip wasn't just taking the guns; he wanted me as well.

The smell of stale beer and piss hit me the moment I was shoved through the door. The place reeked of men, and I felt sick to my stomach. There were too many inside, for me to try to leave. I didn't want to get set on by a pack of outlaws. The rest of the Hawks stood aside and watched me being pushed into the downstairs office.

Besty shut the door behind him and then held his hand out.

"Keys, phone, and weapons now," he ordered.

I gave him my phone and the keys to the van, then I reached into the back pocket of my jeans and pulled out my switch blade.

"Fetch," I said and threw it across the floor.

He wasn't impressed. After retrieving my knife, he ran at me, brought his fist up, and punched me in the stomach. I fell groaning to the floor.

Reaching, he grabbed hold of the collar of my jacket and pulled me up. He threw me against the desk and then started to undo my jeans.

"Get your fucking hands off me!" I screamed and struggled, but he leaned forward so I was squashed between the edge of the desk and his body.

"Trip's not gonna be happy about this," I warned.

"You're not his old' lady anymore and I'll take what I want when I want. And you know how much I want you," he panted.

"Don't touch me!" I yelled while struggling to move under his weight.

"Don't be like that, you little cock teaser," he hissed as he undid my jeans and pulled them down with my knickers and then pushed me over the table, so I was lying across it.

"You still like it hard and fast," he growled.

I heard the tinkle of his belt buckle and knew he was about to enter me.

Before I could scream out, his greasy-smelling hand covered my mouth and made me gag.

"Shut the fuck up," he whispered. I felt him turn his body toward the door and then a blade of a knife piercing the skin of my throat.

I wondered if Trip knew what was happening, how he would react if he found out Besty was raping me. I assumed Trip would want me first before handing me over to someone else. Maybe I should get his attention and find out. Somehow, I had to make enough noise to alert them outside.

He pushed himself deep inside and started rocking. His hand that held the knife moved about an inch away from my neck. I slowly reached my arm across the table to try to grab for something, but Besty had my head held down and I couldn't turn to see what I was grabbing at. He was too much in the moment to notice my hand reaching. Groaning and panting, his thrusts picked up speed. I blocked out the noise of his obscene fucking and concentrated on getting my hand around what felt like a cup. I had two choices, I could try to throw it at the door, hoping to get the Hawks' attention or I could whack the motherfucker over the head with it. I doubted my aim was good enough to make the door, so I made sure I had a good grip of the cup. Bending, I used all my force and smashed it in his face. I couldn't reach his head. Besty staggered back, covering his right eye with his hand while blood seeped between his fingers.

I took a deep breath and screamed as he lunged, cursing at me.

Road Rage

The door swung open. The biker stared at the scene. He looked at me first and then at Besty, who immediately reached down to pull up his pants and jeans. I realised I was standing naked from the waist down. Picking my clothes off the floor, I crawled further away from them both and started to dress.

"Umm - Trip wants you," the biker said.

"Give me a sec," Besty answered as he tried to stem the flow of blood.

"He said now," the biker dared to argue.

Neither of them looked at me as I watched them leave. I waited until I saw the door close and heard the key turn in the lock before crumbling to the floor.

Pushing myself up into a sitting position, I wiped away the fallen tears. I was hurting. My chest felt like it had been crushed and coughing only seemed to worsen it. I saw the Iron Maiden cup broken in two pieces on the floor and wept even harder. Iron Maiden was my favourite rock band, and I worshipped those guys. I felt gutted that I'd broken the cup. A stupid reaction I know, but I think I was in shock.

I crawled across the dark blue mat and over to the threadbare couch located at the far wall, trying not to think about how many times I'd been fucked on it.

As I lay holding my stomach, I cursed my stupidity. Things had not gone to plan. I knew that a bruised body wouldn't be the only injury I'd sustain by the hand of the Hawks. I knew what was coming, but I couldn't think about that for now. I had to concentrate on finding a way out of the dangerous situation I was in.

I couldn't try to talk my way out of it. I knew that when Trip made up his mind there was no changing it. Maybe I should give myself to him in return for my freedom? I shook my head. No. There was no way I could do that, not even if my life depended on it, I thought stubbornly. Perhaps I'd be lucky, and Rage would come looking for me; only I knew I shouldn't count on them. They'd be fools if they did.

My only hope was to try and escape if the chance presented itself.

I heard the key turn in the lock. My heart raced as the door opened.

"Pope!" I cried.

Finally, a friendly face. Even though he'd shaved off his goatee, he still looked the same. Deep blue eyes and large pink lips took up most of his face. His nose was long but thin. The sides of his shaggy black hair were tucked behind his ears like he always wore it.

The Hawk smiled before closing the door behind him.

"I thought you could do with a drink," he said as he put the neck of the bottle between his teeth and pulled off the cap.

"Thanks," I said and reached out for it.

"Jesus, Ford, what the hell are you doing back here?" he asked as he offered me the joint he'd just lit up. Then he sat down beside me on the couch.

"Long story and a fucking big mistake," I answered, and then took a grateful drag.

Pope had been a close friend to me back in my Hawk days. We'd been through some wars together and I trusted him. I hoped he'd still be loyal to me.

"The good life suits you," he said. "But you look too good. You know Trip's walking 'round the club with a hard-on."

I smiled tightly.

"I'm surprised you're still running with them," I said.

"Yeah well, old habits die hard."

I took a swig of beer then looked down to the floor.

Gently, he raised my head and turned my neck to see the knife wound. "Did he hurt you?"

"Yes, but I've had worse."

He nodded his head.

"Did Trip say anything to him?" I asked.

"Why should he?" he shrugged.

"Yeah," I answered. "I saw the patch. How long has the

bastard been VP?"

"Awhile. You watch yourself around him. You know he's got a thing for you."

I bowed my head. "Fuck, what am I gonna do, Pope?"

"Don't look at me, hon. You're gonna have to figure out this one yourself. Christ. What the fuck did you think would happen?"

I took another long drag of the joint and nodded my head in agreement. I was an idiot to think the deal would have gone smoothly.

"My hands are tied," he continued. "The good news is Trip's left instructions that you're not to be touched. Talking of which, don't think he'd be too pleased about me being here with you."

He stood up to leave. I grabbed his arm.

"Wait. Is there nothing you can do?"

He shook his head.

"Can you at least get a message to Rage. Tell them what's happened?"

"No fucking way!"

He patted my arm gently. "I'm sorry, Ford, but you're on your own."

"It's Gemma," I screamed as the door closed behind him.

I sat back down on the couch, hugging my knees to my chest while the bottle dangled from my hands. I never thought of Pope as a way out. I didn't expect to see him still with them. If only I could talk with him again, get him to see sense. But I knew I would be asking too much. Why should he put himself in danger for me?

The only sound I could hear was the smashing of the cue ball, and it was an eerie and lonely sound. I ached for company or just the sound of muffled talking, so I wouldn't feel so alone. I lay down on the couch and stared at the paint-cracked ceiling, wondering what was going to happen next.

It was around four in the afternoon when I got a visit from Trip. He came in and threw a The Meat Locker bag onto my lap.

"Can't have my guest starving, can I?" he sniggered.

The smell of the burger woke my appetite and I greedily tucked in.

Trip pulled a chair over and sat in front of me, watching me eat. He couldn't keep the smile off his fucking face.

"How long have you been an officer with Rage?" he asked.

I stopped chewing and swallowed what was in my mouth. My eyes ran tears as I choked away the meat.

"What are you talking about?" I managed to splutter.

"Only an officer would be sent on a weapon drop. So, Ford, how long?"

"Stop calling me Ford," I yelled.

The burger fell from my fingers as he gripped my wrist tightly. "How long?" he barked.

"About a year," I answered, and then pulled my hand away.

He smiled and sat back down watching me chew my fries.

Trip waited until I finished eating then he sat on the couch beside me. Gripping my chin, he turned my head, so I was facing him and then gently stroked the new scar on my face.

"Still playing rough?" he sniggered.

"No, a man attacked me."

"Who? Who did this to you?" he demanded as though he gave a shit and was going to sort out the guy. Jesus, the man just allowed his VP to rape me.

"It's sorted. Rage took care of the guy. He's not around anymore."

Big mistake! God, I wanted to swallow my tongue. Now I made Rage sound as though they were in the same league as the Hawks.

He leaned in to kiss me, but I pushed him away.

"Get your fucking hands off me!" I shouted.

"Now, don't be like that," he smiled and grabbed at my breasts. "You've no idea how much I've missed you." He breathed huskily.

Road Rage

"You can't have me," I said and stood up.

He pulled me back down and gripping my chin, forced me to look into his face.

I pulled my head away. "Hell will freeze over before I give myself to you."

Leaning in close, he whispered. "I'm gonna break you, slowly. I don't care how long it takes. I'm gonna keep stripping away at this hard shell until you're vulnerable again."

Raising my hand, I used all my strength to punch him in the face.

He rubbed his jaw and laughed. "I'll let that one slide."

Standing up, with his hands on his hip, he looked down at me.

"I want you in the bar later. We're having a party."

A clubhouse party meant either a Hawk had been released from jail, or it was a patch over.

"Look, Trip, take the guns, but let me go. I don't want to be here I have a good life back home, and a man who loves me. I'm not Ford anymore; that person died a long time ago. Don't expect me to feel at home with this situation. Things have changed and I don't party anymore."

"You look different," he said, "but you're still tough, and the anger remains no matter how much you try to suppress it."

He knew me too well.

"Be a good girl tonight. Behave and do what you're told, smile and make everyone happy and I'll think about letting you go."

"I'm not going to be anyone's plaything," I declared.

"I won't let any Hawk rough you up; you have my word on that. Look, you've landed on my doorstep, and I want to spend time with you. Is that too much to ask for?"

It was too good to be true. All I had to do was behave that evening, keep his company and then he would let me go? I doubted it was that easy.

"Okay, if you promise me, you won't hurt me, and you'll let me go tomorrow."

"That's my girl," he smiled. "You've got a long night ahead, get some rest; I'll make sure no one disturbs you again. Oh, and make sure you wear your jacket tonight. It will be good for the others to see the association our two clubs have."

What association? I thought. So not all the Hawks knew I was a captive.

"Umm, don't suppose I can use the toilet before you lock me in?"

"Of course," Trip laughed. "Where's my manners? You know where they are."

I walked past him, opened the door, and walked towards the toilets that were situated off the right of the worn, dark wooden bar. A soiled pool table took up most of the room while torn, plastic covered stools lined the bar. The Hawks watched me as I passed. Besty sat on a bar stool, holding an ice pack to his cut and swollen eye. He scowled and mouthed the words, "Later bitch."

I pushed open the door to the toilet and then sighed with relief. I didn't realise I'd been holding my breath since I left the office. I looked at my reflection in the rusty and broken mirror. The left corner of my lip was cut, which gave me a hardened appearance. My hair was tangled and looked a mess. But what did I care about how I looked? In fact, I deemed it would be better for my safety if I looked a mess. I had no idea what Trip had planned for me that night, but there was no way to escape. As freedom was only a few hours away, I told myself I could get through it. I sat down and thought of Doc. He'd be expecting me home by now and would worry. I thought about what Blade would think about me not phoning in. Would they act?

I didn't stay long in the toilet. Trip was in the bar when I returned. I didn't look at him; I just walked straight into the office and closed the door. A minute later, I heard the door lock.

I lay on the couch, but sleep wouldn't come as I tried

Road Rage

to picture what was happening outside. I fantasied about a rescue by Rage that I knew would never happen, but it comforted me, nonetheless. I jumped when I heard the door open. I sat up, as light from the noisy bar lit up the office. I looked down at my watch it was eight thirty and from the sound of it, the club house was quickly filling up.

A lady Hawk stood in the doorway. "Trip wants you to tidy yourself up," she said. "I brought you your things." She threw my bag down by the couch and then turned on the office light before closing the door again. This time, it wasn't locked. I sat up and rubbed my eyes before pulling the bag up onto the couch. I had no intention of changing my clothes, I was quite happy to stink of sweat, but I knew Trip would expect me to wear makeup and make an effort. I didn't want to antagonise the bastard, so I combed the tangles out of my hair and then pinned it up. I never carried much make up on me, so I used what I had. I covered my lips lightly with my copper lipstick and then drew a line across my eye with a black pencil. I only had a hand mirror with me so I couldn't see the full effects. I hoped it wasn't too much. I didn't want the others getting a hard-on for me as well.

I wasn't going to wait for a Hawk to come marching into the office and escort me out like some prisoner, so I walked out into the bar by myself.

Thankfully, no one took much notice of me, and the volume of laughter and chatter stayed the same. I walked over to the bar and asked for a beer. I watched carefully as the Hawk pulled the top off a bottle of Bud and handed it to me. I never saw him slip anything in, so I guzzled it down gratefully. I turned, leaned against the bar, and looked around. I caught Trip's eye and he raised his bottle in a toast. I ignored him and my eyes continued to search the room. They fell onto Pope, and I smiled, but it was soon cut off as Besty's face came into view. He stood in front of me. I straightened up, and my fists clenched at my sides.

"Get the fuck out of my face," I warned.

Grabbing hold of my arm, he leaned toward me, ready to say something, when Trip's voice rang out.

"Come and join us," he called to me.

I pushed past Besty and walked over to the table.

"Tiny, Dodge, this is Ford. You know Pope, of course."

"She used to run with us," Pope explained.

I smiled to him, nodded to the two Hawks and then sat on the vacant seat.

"You were Trip's old' lady?" Tiny asked.

I cringed at the word. "Yes, I was, but that was a long time ago." I turned my head and took a swig of my beer.

"So, you're with Rage now?" Dodge asked. "I've seen them on the circuit. They're good."

I looked at Trip before saying. "Yes, we are."

Dodge lit up a joint and then offered it to me. I didn't want to get high, especially as I needed to keep my guard up, but Trip nodded his head slightly, so I took it, inhaled a couple of drags and then handed it back.

"What are you doing down this way?" Tiny answered.

Trip started up a conversation with the other Hawks and I sat back listened and scanned the room.

The lady Hawks were partying hard, dancing sexily with hardly any clothes on. What with the smells of testosterone, stale beer and skank and the sounds of bottles clinking, laughter and the same rock songs playing the background, I felt as though I'd never left the place. I smiled in spite of myself. I knew I was getting stoned. I took another drag of a fresh joint and then passed it to Tiny.

Besty came over and stood beside me. "You wanna dance?" he said.

I couldn't believe the nerve of the guy. Did he think I was high or something?

"Go fuck yourself," I spat.

He shrugged and walked away while laughter echoed around the table.

"Bet the place hasn't changed to you?" Trip asked me.

Road Rage

I wanted to say, "No it's the same shit hole I remember," but instead I replied, "No it hasn't."

"You remember when Stony got out of prison, you blew every guy in the place that night," Trip laughed.

"No, I don't. I was high on coke, remember that?" I retorted.

"You wanna shoot some pool?" Troy asked.

"Not the kind you have in mind," I said and smiled as I thought back to how every game of pool with a female ended up as strip pool.

I looked over my shoulder and it seemed the game was already heading that way. Five Hawks were standing around the table while two women were playing. Leaning over the table to take their shot, they stuck their arses up in the air deliberately. Wolf whistles drowned out the noise of the shot. I turned back around and slowly shook my head.

"You sure I can't persuade you?" Troy asked and grinned.

"I'll pass," I answered, and quickly glanced at Trip who was smiling. If he ordered me to play, I'd have no choice but to undress in front of the whole club. Thankfully, Trip seemed satisfied to just sit and watch. Troy soon left the table and wandered over to see the show, which was getting rowdier by the minute. I knew how the game would play out and I was thankful that my back was turned from the scene.

Trip patted his knee, indicating for me to go over. I did what I was told and sat on his lap. He held me tightly around the waist and nuzzled his face into my neck. Years ago, I would have surrendered to his advances, but now his touch and breath made my skin crawl. I wanted Doc's arms around me, not that scumbag's.

The takeout finally arrived, and I was starving, but Trip was holding me firmly and unless he was eating, I wasn't going to get any food.

By twelve, the place was packed. The volume of laughter and music seemed to increase the more they snorted and smoked. We were still seated so I couldn't see anything but a sea of leather and blue jeans. I stuck to beer and a couple of joints. I refused the coke that was offered. I wasn't in that game anymore. Throughout the evening, more Hawks joined our table and Trip would disappear to the other side of the room to chat with his brothers. I relaxed a little when he left, but I never dropped my guard and I only spoke when someone directed their question at me. Tiny and Dodge seemed friendly enough, but I knew that would change if they learnt that I was there against my will.

The Hawks were a close family. Bonded by their love for motorcycles and violence, they stuck by each other and never backed down. I knew I couldn't rely on the two Hawks to help me out, so I carried on the charade. I had a few smiles and greetings from other Hawks, who I assumed were from a different chapter and didn't know what was going on. Apart from Besty, Troy and Pope, Trip's chapter never made any contact with me. It was as though I wasn't even in the room. I saw Pope keeping a sly watch on me, but I knew he wouldn't be able to help me if something kicked off. I refused to get caught up with the energetic ambience. I just wanted to be home, safe with my man.

It was nearing one in the morning when Trip came up to me at the bar where I was waiting to get served. He leaned his body onto mine. I felt his erection. I tried to push him away, but he grabbed my wrist and whispered close to my ear.

"We can do this two ways; either you come with me, and I fuck you, or I'll get some friends to join us, and I promise you a night you will never forget."

I didn't have any other choice. I knew from past experience what Trip's sex parties were like. I walked towards the office with Trip following close behind. I caught Pope's eye and heard sniggers, as Trip turned on the light and then shut the office door.

"Get undressed," he ordered.

I did what he said and stood in front of him waiting for

Road Rage

his next command. Trip stared at me, eyeing my body. I thought he was waiting for me to undress completely when he said, "Lay down on the floor."

I knew that begging and pleading with him to stop would only excite him more, so I lay back and looked at the ceiling while I heard him unbuckle his Harley Davidson belt and unzip his jeans.

"I can't do this, David." It was barely a whisper, but my words stopped Trip in his tracks. He pushed himself off me and sat kneeling with his hand on his hips.

"What did you say?" he stared at me for what seemed like an eternity. No one called him by his real name.

I didn't repeat myself, just turned my head away from him and kept silent.

"You've changed and I don't like it," he said. "Not to worry, I've got time to wait. Open your fucking legs next time, you'll enjoy it."

I sat up and yelled, "You said you'd let me go!"

"And you said you'd behave and do what you were told. I guess we both have been fucked tonight," he sniggered.

I knew it was over when he pulled up his jeans and stood up.

"Trip, wait. I'm sorry. I'm ready now." I lay back down and opened my legs wide.

He laughed gruffly. "No, thanks. There's plenty of fresh pussy for me outside. I don't need dirty seconds."

I watched him walk back out, and it took a lot of control to stop from jumping on his back and clawing his eyes out.

Talk about humiliation. There I was, almost naked, unwillingly giving my body to a man I hated the most, and then he rejected me. I felt used, ashamed and dirty. As I dressed, I allowed the tears to fall, but then came the anger.

I was seething, anger so intense I thought it would burn me alive. Pacing the room, I flung my arm across the table, throwing everything on the floor. I ripped posters and pictures from the wall, smashing and ripping them to pieces. It felt good to release the rage. I was nowhere finished with my destruction when three Hawks came rushing into the room. They threw me to the ground and held me down while Besty stuck a needle in my neck.

I woke up to darkness. I didn't know where I was, but the ground was cold and smelt damp. Waiting until my eyes adjusted to the darkness, I then realised I was in the barn next to the clubhouse. I recognised the same skeleton relics of bikes that the barn always housed. My head felt foggy. It took a moment to realise I'd been drugged. I reached down and touched my legs, relieved that I was still dressed. The leather jacket I was still wearing did nothing to comfort me from the early morning chill. There wasn't enough light in the barn to see my watch clearly, so I had no idea how late it was. Pushing myself off the floor, I walked over to the two large, wooden barn doors. Peered through the small gaps of the rotting wood, I saw two Hawks standing in front of the barn, talking quietly to one another.

"Hey," I called. No response. "Oy you," I yelled louder, finally getting their attention. I moved away while they opened the door. Both stood in front of me blocking my exit.

"I'm hungry. I want some bloody food. And tell Trip I want to speak with him."

"He's not here," one answered.

"Keep quiet and I'll get you some grub," the other said, and then they turned and left.

I waited until my eyes adjusted to the darkness again and then I looked for somewhere to sit. I was cold enough without having to sit on the ground again.

I'm not sure how much time passed before I heard the scrunching of feet on the gravel outside. The same two guards opened the barn door. One handed me my breakfast—The Meat Locker takeout again—and the other threw a brown, grotty looking blanket down at my feet.

"I need the toilet," I said, hoping I wasn't pushing my luck.

"Use the coke cup," one replied and then sniggered.

Road Rage

"You can't fucking keep me locked up here!" I shouted.

Walking back outside, they ignored my continued verbal abuse.

I sat down and scoffed the burger and fries. I was so hungry that after I finished, my stomach still rumbled. Even though my throat was parched, I tipped the coke on the floor.

I didn't think I was going to be disturbed again that night, so I settled on the floor. Using my jacket as a pillow, I wrapped the musty-smelling blanket around me. Even after what I'd been through and being awake for over twenty-four hours, I still couldn't sleep. As I lay, looking at the ceiling, a memory came rushing into my head. The day that changed my life.

***

I had just turned fifteen, an innocent but inquisitive fifteen-year-old. It was a sunny morning in July. I woke up feeling rested and happy as I watched the sunlight doing its best to burst into the bedroom. It was the school holidays, so normally I would snuggle under the quilt for a few more minutes, only the sun was screaming at me to bathe in its rays. My mother had already left for work, and as I loved walking in the sunshine, I decided to go down to the High Street bank and deposit my month's paper-round money. I popped into the bakery and bought a tasty, sugary cream doughnut, which I ate while browsing the shop's windows. The traffic was heavy and the road busy with shoppers, but that didn't stop me from swinging my bag to the rhythm of the tune I was humming. To make my morning even better, there were only a few customers inside the bank. I guessed I would be in and out in ten minutes.

I'd been in the bank queuing for five minutes when five men dressed in black, along with balaclavas, came bursting through the doors. They reminded me of SAS guys I'd seen on TV, what with the black balaclava that covered most of his face. However, the machine guns that hung around their necks made the situation real. They didn't need to announce it was a hold up; it was obvious to us they weren't going to a fancy dress party.

"You touch that button, and it will be the last thing you do," an angry voice called out. "All the staff to the back wall, facing me," he instructed.

I then had a gun pointed at me and I was ordered to lie face down on the floor. We did as we were told. These guys didn't act as though they were playing games and we didn't want to give them an excuse to get trigger happy. When you're faced with reality, you forget all about grabbing a gun and kicking the guy in the balls. Truthfully, you do as you're told, when you're told it. I heard the clerks filling up what I assumed were money bags. I told myself it would soon be over. They would get what they came for and leave peacefully without anyone getting hurt.

Only it didn't happen like that. One of the bank staff must have pushed the silent alarm because I heard sirens, then cars sliding to a halt outside the bank. Doors banged shut and then there was silence.

Knowing the police were outside should have given me hope, but I was a smart fifteen-year-old. Now, instead of us being customers in the wrong place at the wrong time, we were hostages in a deadly situation.

I expected to hear a surge of panic between the robbers, only they were calm and silent, carrying on with the job at hand as though they hadn't even heard the sirens. I waited to hear the police outside on the loudspeaker, but it never came. Instead, I heard a thump and lifted my head in time to see a male clerk get a second punch from one of the gunmen.

"Try that again, motherfucker," he warned.

"Keep your head down or I'll blow the fucker off."

I wasn't the only one having a look. The warning didn't sound like an empty threat. I think it was then that I finally realised they could kill us all and not think twice about it.

I'm going to die, I thought, and tears ran down my face.

Road Rage

Stop it! You're going to get through this. Just do as they say and you won't get hurt, I lectured.

The silence in the bank was really scary. I wondered what they were waiting for. The money had been collected and the clerks stood with their backs against the wall. The five gunmen remained in their positions, not saying a word, a silent stand-off, which was suddenly broken by the ringing of a phone. A couple of us cried out in alarm. I know I jumped.

"Reaper, take the hostages over there," a voice commanded. He pointed to the place with the muzzle of his gun.

The robber named Reaper cocked the machine gun, making us all jump again.

"You heard the man," he yelled. "Get moving over there."

I stood up and looked to where the gunman was pointing and quietly followed everyone else. One of the hostages, an older man, wasn't walking fast enough for Reaper's liking, and so he grabbed him by the arm and shoved him across the shiny marble floor.

We were now standing in a crowded circle in the middle of the bank. I counted eight of us. Three other women, I, three men and a small boy who hung onto his mother tightly. I wished I had my mum with me, but then the thought faded, and I was glad she was safe at work.

"Get down onto your knees and put your hands behind your head," Reaper ordered.

Again, we did as we were told. The floor was cold and hard, and it hurt to kneel, but I wasn't about to complain. At last, I was able to have a good look around.

All of the staff had been rounded up and were standing against the back wall behind the teller desks. The security door that separated the staff from the public had been propped open by a chair. One of the gunmen stood beside the staff, his gun poised in his hands. I looked at the man standing next to me. Both hands were on his gun, his feet slightly apart. And the way he stood made me think of a soldier. The two other gunmen, one that stood beside the main door and the other by the far window, positioned themselves in the same military fashion. One hand, held the gun muzzle, the other hand was on the trigger. I came to the conclusion that either they were ex-soldiers, or they had pulled so many bank jobs that they had their own code of conduct. I then turned my attention to the gunman who was speaking on the phone. Unfortunately, his attention was also focused on me. He was talking calmly to someone on the other line. I felt his stare burn, so I quickly looked down at the floor.

The head gunman--well, I assumed he was as he was the one negotiating on the phone--walked over to Reaper. Before he spoke, he stared again at me. All I could see were dark eyes and pink lips that seemed to scowl. My eyes quickly found the floor again.

"Let these ones go, we have enough to negotiate with."

The gunman behind the counter called out, "What do we get in return, Panther?"

"Anything we want. Shadow, get the key to the door. I wanna lock this baby up tight."

"Might as well go the whole hog," the gunman by the door called out.

"Good idea," Panther answered. "Spider, get the manager to open the safe."

I watched Spider leave his post and go behind the counter. I breathed a sigh of relief. It seemed as though we were free to go, but I pitied the staff that were left behind.

We were ordered to stand up and walk towards the door with our hands on our heads. I was fourth in line and stupidly decided to have another look around the bank. I wanted to be able to give a good description to the police. All the gunmen were around the same build and although most of their face and body were covered, I managed to find something different about each of them. I finished my scan and then turned my head back round to the front when Panther called out. "Stop her."

I knew he was referring to me. I was only a few meters

away from freedom, so I ran for the door. I managed to grab hold of the handle before a butt of a gun came crashing down onto my skull. I swear I saw stars as the floor came to meet me and the world turned black.

When I woke, I was laying on a couch inside an office. I was alone, the door was shut and, I assumed, locked. To say I felt sick was an understatement. I closed my eyes hoping that the dizziness would cease. My head hurt, the pain causing me to feel sick. I was so angry with myself. If I had kept me head down and done what I was told, I'd be home, safe. But I had to be nosy; even after Panther had noticed me looking around, I didn't stop. You stupid cow, I cursed. I would have said the words out loud, only I couldn't open my mouth as I had tape stuck across. And I couldn't pull it off as my hands were tied tightly behind my back. I knew I was in serious trouble and this time, I allowed the tears to fall.

I can't guess how long I lay on the couch. My head ached, I had pains in my arms, but I was determined I wasn't going to cry anymore. I waited until I was calmer and then stood myself up. I wondered what was happening outside. Had they gone? Was everything finished? Had they forgotten about me? I found a digital clock on the desk. It read one fifteen. I remembered entering the bank at quarter to nine. Jesus, I must have been unconscious for hours, I thought. The missing time gave me even more hope that the robbery was over. I couldn't hear anything outside the door and the curtained window didn't give much away. I had no idea where the office was situated within the bank; I could have been upstairs for all I knew. I also wondered if anyone else had been hurt. Their words weren't empty threats. I kept getting reminded every time my head throbbed.

It was three thirty when I finally heard a noise outside, a shadow walked past the window. Then I heard the keys turn in the lock.

I was sitting on the couch, hoping in hell it was one of

the staff, or a policeman coming to rescue me. My hopes were dashed as one of the gunmen walked into the room I was surprised to see him as I truly believed it was over. The gunman called Reaper walked straight towards me and slowly pulled off the tape. The glue took off most of the skin from my lips. Tears ran down my face and I felt blood dripping down my chin.

"Time to eat, honey," he said cheerfully, and pushed me onto my side.

He knelt on my legs as he untied my hands, then reached into his pocket and pulled out a squashed sandwich and threw it at me. Food was the last thing on my mind, but I guessed the police didn't want us hostages to starve. I rubbed my sore wrists which were now red with burn marks.

"I guess things aren't going to plan," I don't know what made me say it. I think I was lonely and needed conversation, even if it meant talking to a dangerous gunman.

"Everything is under control. Nothing to worry your pretty head about," he answered calmly.

"Why am I still here? Please let me go," I begged.

"Too much curiosity," he answered. "What's your name?"

"Gemma."

"And you know who I am?" he asked, his eyes widened waiting for my response.

"You're called Reaper"

"Oh, you're good," he said smiling. "Eat," he ordered, pointing the gun at the sandwich.

I took a bite and was surprised how good it tasted.

I was thinking of something to say, something cautious, when Reaper spoke first.

"It won't be long now. You'll soon be home. How old are you?

"Fifteen."

"No fucking way," he gasped.

I was tall for my age with long legs. I knew I looked older than I was.

Road Rage

"Thought you were at least eighteen," he said.

"What's happening out there?" I asked.

"Panther's still talking to the cops. We've got our transport; he's just taking his time, making them sweat."

"But you're not sweating," I replied.

"You sure you're only fifteen?" He smiled.

Reaper waited patiently for me to finish eating, and then he re-tied my hands behind my back and taped over my mouth. I sat and let him, without a struggle. I wasn't giving them any more reasons to hurt me.

"Panther will be in to see you soon. He wants to introduce himself properly."

I didn't get the meaning. I didn't understand.

He then left without another word. After the door locked, I relaxed a little. A few minutes later I heard the familiar tinkling of the lock.

Panther entered the room. The sudden change in atmosphere scared me. The moment he walked inside the air became tense, and I felt frightened for my life.

He took the chair from behind the desk and pulled it over to the couch. He sat down and stared at me. His legs were crossed, and his arms folded. I stared back. Two can play at that game, I thought.

Then he shocked me by removing his balaclava. My eyes quickly found the floor, but even that wasn't enough. I turned my head away from him. I didn't want to see his face.

Panther gave a cold chuckle. "Not so curious now, are you?" he spat. "Look at me, bitch!" he yelled.

I knew that if I looked at him, saw exactly was he looked like; I would be signing my own death warrant.

"You're a little too nosy for my liking. I've been watching you taking everything in, ready to tell the cops."

I shook my head and mumbled a denial, still not daring to look at him. Panther laughed.

"Look at me," he ordered. "It's rude not to look at someone when they're speaking to you."

But nothing would make me turn my head.

I started crying, I couldn't help it. I wasn't strong. I was weak, and I didn't care if I showed my weakness. Why would he reveal his true identity to me if they were going to let me go? I was going to die, I knew it.

"My name is Panther, Gemma, as you very well know. I've been watching you and I like what I see, so I've come to get to know you better. Look at me!"

I jumped, but I wouldn't face him.

He leapt off the chair and grabbed me by my hair, pulling my head back until I had no choice but to look. I knew it was over for me.

Once Panther got what he wanted, he pushed me back against the couch and returned to his seat. There didn't seem any point in turning away now, so I faced him. He was in his early thirties, dark eyes, with blonde streaked short hair, which stuck to his face. He had a long tribal style tattoo painted on his left cheek. The smile he was wearing made me feel sick.

The door to the office opened. Spider came in.

"The cops are on the phone again. They say we're running out of time," Spider announced. I allowed a second of relief at the thought of Panther leaving.

"Ignore it," Panther ordered. "And don't interrupt me; I'm going to be busy for the next fifteen minutes."

My heart was beating so fast I thought I'd pass out. Spider was standing at the door staring at Panther. I tried to make eye contact with him, but he wouldn't acknowledge me. I think Spider understood then that I wouldn't be leaving the place alive. He retreated, closing the door quietly behind him.

I didn't want to acknowledge what was about to happen. But as I was tied and gagged, there was nothing I could do to stop it.

Panther pulled the strap of the gun over his head and sat the weapon down on the floor beside him. He stood up and then knelt down by the couch; he parted my legs so he could sit in between. I struggled and muffled out screams as he raped me. The look of hunger in his face forced me to close my eyes. I couldn't watch, although I felt and heard everything, and I will never forget the grunting sounds he made as he rocked and pushed himself inside of me. I remember how upset I felt at the thought of losing my virginity to a rapist and not to a boy I loved.

I cried, I screamed, I gagged and choked, but every sound I made seemed to excite him further. He came really quickly, but it wasn't over for me. He got himself excited again real fast. When he was ready, he grabbed me by my arm, and dragged me over to the desk. With one sweep of his hand, he cleared away the clutter and then pushed me down. Lifting my right leg up until my foot rested on his shoulder, he entered me. The penetration was deep, and I cried out loud. I honestly thought my insides were splitting.

I felt him shudder, heard him cry out, and then he fell limp on top of me. His weight crushed my arms further. Oh, the intense pain, I cried.

"Bet you fucking enjoyed that, didn't you? You needed a good shag," Panther told me, as he zipped up his fly.

I slid off the desk and stood up shaking. Was it over? Was he going to kill me now, I wondered? He pulled his balaclava over his face, and then pushed me back over to the couch. He hung his gun around his neck and then pointed it straight at me. This is it, I thought. Oh, God, help me.

"Raven is coming to see you next. Be a good girl and you might live to see another day," he told me.

It wasn't over. My nightmare was just beginning. Was I going to meet each of them, face to face? The thought of being raped again made me want to die. I can't deal with this. What have I done to deserve this?

My heart pounded and sweat ran down my neck. I wasn't given long to panic as Panther had only just left when the door was being unlocked again. Raven stepped inside.

My arms were still tied behind my back, and I guess that my right arm was broken, as I couldn't move it without causing shooting pains down my side. The injury didn't stop me jumping off the couch and running to the far end of the office. Raven pulled off his balaclava, revealing a greasy black-haired man in his forties, with a greedy smile. He started walking towards me. I was backed up against the wall, so I tried to dodge him, hoping to get to the unlocked door. My attempt didn't get far.

Raven grabbed hold of my injured arm. The pain was so intense I collapsed into his arms. He laid me on the floor and got on top of me right away. He stunk of sweat and his weight crushed my arms further. I barely remained conscious as he raped me. Luckily it was over quickly, and he dressed and left without saying a word.

I stayed on the floor, lying on my side in a foetal position. I wished I was dead. I don't know how long I lay there for, as I couldn't see the clock.

It was while Shadow was brutally raping me that the police finally stormed the bank. Panther and two others were killed in the gun battle. The bank staff escaped unhurt.

As for me, no amount of therapy was going to return my innocence I had lost that the moment I entered the bank. The only way I could deal with what happened to me was to blank everything out and be angry with the world. The following year flashed by in a blur. I allowed my relationship with my parents and friends to deteriorate, and it didn't bother me one bit. I knew then I had to get away.

I'd been living with the Hawks for a few months when I came across numerous black SAS costumes hidden in a box in a store cupboard at their club house. There was no mistaking the black combat trousers, jumpers and balaclavas. And when I asked, no one hid the truth.

I knew then that is was the Hawks who were the gunmen in the bank the sunny July morning. And it was the Hawks that took away my teenage years. Only, by then, I was too fucked up to care about the implications. Settled in a lifestyle of drugs and abuse, I felt I belonged there and deserved everything they dished out.

Doc didn't know about what happened at the bank and I never talked to him about the shame that continued to eat me up inside. I brushed away the tears and hid my head under the grotty blanket. I sobbed loudly and my body shook as I fought to control my emotions. Eventually, I exhausted myself enough to fall asleep.

The roar of motorbikes woke me. I threw off the blanket and put my jacket back on, hoping it would warm my chilled arms. As I put my hands into the pocket, I felt my lighter. I'd forgotten I had it. My cigarettes were still in the inside pocket. I looked up to the beamed cobwebbed roof and said, "Thank you." I'm not an over religious person but when luck comes your way you have to thank someone.

I savoured the burning and the dizziness the nicotine caused. A thought occurred to me. I could start a fire, burn the fucking place down, but then I imagined myself still trapped inside. Knowing Trip, he'd let me burn to death. Soon after the thought left, Trip came in to see me.

"Did you sleep well?" he greeted.

I scowled at him.

"I heard you were asking for me. Did you get lonely?" he laughed.

I didn't like the way he was staring down at me, so I stood up

"You've had your fun. Now let me go."

"I haven't even started yet. Something occurred to me last night..."

That's highly unlikely, I thought. The guy didn't have an ounce of sense.

"Those racers you run with; I wonder how much they'd pay to have you back."

I couldn't find the words and so stared at him open mouthed.

"Yeah," he continued. "I'm thinking with all the expensive

bikes they ride, these guys must have money right? You're important to them - an officer. The question is how much are you worth?"

"Nothing," I answered. "They won't pay anything. You're barking up the wrong tree. I'm nobody."

"You'll never be a nobody, Ford."

"You're not serious about this. Trip, this is madness. Ransom! Just let me go, okay?"

Before he could answer, a Hawk came into the barn and informed him he had an urgent phone call.

I was locked up again, the daylight shut out.

I'd never known the Hawks to kidnap anyone, but now I wouldn't put anything past Trip.

As I waited for him to return, I heard a commotion outside. Running to the door, I peered through the gaps in the wood to see what was going on.

Trip and the other officers were barking orders while Hawks were running to their bikes and taking off. Something was going down, and I was eager to find out what it was.

I was lucky enough to overhear a snippet of conversation between the two Hawks stationed outside the barn. For some reason or other, the mother chapter was coming down on an inspection. I hoped someone had tipped them off to what was happening down in the south. Although the club had their hands in most illegal activities, I didn't see them as being too happy about Trip's kidnapping and ransom exploits.

If Trip had any sense, he'd have me moved, and I knew that if that happened, it would be my only chance for escape. I had to form a plan.

The lot was emptying fast. Bikes roared away and it looked as through the rest of the club, including my guards, had gone into the clubhouse. I ran over to the corner of the barn and started rummaging through a pile of metal junk, hoping to find something to hit out with. I found an old rusty exhaust pipe, but it was too heavy to get a good swing, so I settled for a metal cog. This could do some damage, I thought as I placed it in the centre of my hand.

I ran back to my spying place just in time to see Besty and another Hawk coming my way. I stood to the side of one of the doors, gripped the cog between my fingers and took a deep breath to steady my nerves.

The door opened and the bikers walked through. They paused as their eyes searched for me and I used that time to kick out my leg. My aim was spot on. The Hawk crumbled to the floor groaning. I swung the cog and caught Besty in the face. Then I ran.

I knew if I could get up the lane and onto the main road, I'd have a chance of flagging down a car before the rest of them gave chase.

Unfortunately, I made the mistake of turning my head to check behind me. I tripped over a small rock. I didn't fall but I lost my balance and hurt my ankle. It wasn't enough to stop me, though; I could limp fast enough. Before I had tripped, I'd seen three Hawks jumping onto their bikes. I knew I didn't have much time. I could see the road ahead. I was just starting to hope, when a bike turned into the lane. The Hawk saw me, raced forwards and skidded to a stop, cutting off my route.

I stopped where I was and held my hands up while I waited for the other bikes to reach me. Besty braked sharply, causing the wheels of his bike to grind the dusty gravel road and throw up a cloud of dirt. Throwing the bike down to the ground, he then ran at me. His hand lashed out before I had time to protect myself.

"Where the fuck do you think you're going?" he yelled and then grabbed my arm and started dragging me towards his bike.

Blood was dripping down Besty's neck where I'd sliced his face open with the cog. I wished I'd taken the fucker's eye out.

Pope stood watching, his face unreadable. Silently, I begged him to help me.

The other bikes followed us as we rode back up the

lane towards the clubhouse. I knew I was in trouble, and I didn't want to think how Trip would punish me.

Two of the Hawks dragged me back towards the barn. I struggled, cursing and yelling in their grip. Trip was waiting inside. His arms folded.

The bikers stopped in front of him and tightened their hold while Trip's hand lashed out and hit me around the face. My lips split open, and my cheek stung from the pain.

"You're gonna wish you hadn't done that," he growled.

I just wished my escape had worked.

"Tie her up and gag her."

"No," I screamed, as the Hawks started pulling me away. "Trip, don't do this. Please."

"Wait," he yelled.

The Hawks stopped and turned back around.

"Please, I won't try anything again. I'll do what you say."

"You're pathetic," he spat. "Ford would never beg."

"When you going to get it in your head?" I screamed. "I'm not Ford. She's gone and not fucking coming back!"

"I ain't got time for this shit. Now I'm stressed, and it's up to you to relax me."

Besty forced me to my knees, as Trip stepped forward, undid his belt buckle and pulled down his jeans.

This was a private act, something I enjoyed with Doc, something I would never do to Trip again, or in public.

My head turned as I heard a gun cock. Knowing that Besty could pull the trigger anytime and I'd be dead, what other choice did I have? I didn't want to show my weakness, but I couldn't stop the tears from falling.

Thankfully he didn't last long.

"Swallow it," he ordered.

There was no way I was going to have him inside of me, so when his panting increased and he finally came, I spat the sperm out over his boots.

That's the kind of thing Ford would have done, I thought smugly.

Trip dressed and then stood over me with his hands on his hips.

"You stupid, stubborn bitch," he growled.

He clicked his fingers once and I was lifted off the ground. With a closed fist, Trip punched me in the stomach. My body crippled but the Hawks kept their hold.

"I ain't got time for your games." Turning to Pope he said. "Get rid of her."

Pope didn't move. "What do you want me to do?"

"Tie her up, get her to the garage, then she's all yours. I want the problem taken care of."

Pope stood his ground.

"If you can't do it, I'll find someone else who will," Trip growled.

"I'll drive," Besty said.

Trip nodded his head. I only had to look at Besty's sickly face to know his intent.

"No. Just let me go, please. Don't do this," I begged. But I knew that no amount of pleading was going to make a difference.

Besty was eager to get his hands on me and now, with the president's permission, I knew I was in for a rough time. All I could think about was Doc. How warm and safe I felt when I was in his arms. How he made me laugh and how happy I felt to be alive.

Anger and then fear took over, I screamed cursed and kicked, struggling in their restraint.

"You son of a bitch," I yelled. "You'll never get away with this, fucker. I'm coming for you. I'm gonna cut off your puny dick and ram it down your throat."

"Gag the bitch," Trip shouted, and then walked away with the rest of the Hawks following.

As Besty held my arms behind my back, Pope tied a soiled bandanna over my mouth. The smell and taste of stale sweat made me want to vomit. The two of them started dragging me toward my van. I then understood what Trip had said. He'd just pulled the trigger to my execution. I was a dead woman. All fight left me, and my body sank to the ground. The Hawks held me under the arms and continued dragging me while the heels of my shoes scraped into the earth. The heavy rain that started pelting down mixed with my silent tears, and I couldn't find the effort to wipe them away.

Besty walked to the front of the van as Pope tied my hands behind my back.

"I'm going to help you," he whispered.

I stopped crying and nodded as he pushed me inside. The doors slammed shut and Besty started the van.

The garage was on the outskirts of the town, away from prying eyes. Although it was open to the public, it was owned by the Hawks.

As I sat quietly in the van I wondered how Pope was going to help me. I didn't want to hope; even so, I couldn't help thinking that he was going to save me from a bullet and that I would soon be in Doc's arms.

The van slowed. Besty reversed up the drive and then shut off the engine.

"I'm gonna get rid of the help then we'll get the bitch inside," he said.

Pope stayed seated, staring out of the window screen.

"I called Rage," he whispered. "They're probably already down here by now looking for you."

Relief flooded through me, but I couldn't verbally thank him.

"Now I need to find a fucking way of phoning them to let them know your new location."

"Shop's closed," I heard Besty bark.

Pope turned in his seat and looked me in the eyes.

"I'm sorry for what happens now, but I have to make it look real."

I nodded. But I didn't understand. Was Pope planning to rape me or beat me up just so he looked good? I was going to fight him off. There would be no acting required.

Pope waited until the workers had left before getting

out of the van. The doors slid open, and I climbed out and stood beside a beat-up purple Renault. The odour of petrol and motor fluids filled my lungs. My heart raced as Besty pulled down the shutter door, leaving the three of us staring at one another in silence.

Pope untied the gag and rope and then ordered me to take off my jacket.

"Fuck you!" I answered.

He rushed at me, ripped the jacket off my arms then flung it to the floor. As his hands started groping, I watched Besty take out a knife and slice off my precious Rage patch.

"You can have her first," he said. "I want to take my time with the bitch. Me and Ford have some catching up to do."

Suddenly, a hungry frenzy took over Pope. He slammed me against the wall, ripped open my blouse, and then grabbed my arms. Holding my arms in a vice over the top of my head, he then used the other hand to undo the button of my jeans. Pope then rammed his hands down my knickers as he sucked on my neck.

He was too strong to push off, I cried out for him to stop. My legs kicked out until he forced them open with his knees.

"Yeah, you like that, don't you, bitch?" he panted.

"Give it to the cunt," Besty shouted with excitement.

Pope's hand froze. Turning his head toward Besty he said. "Mind giving me some privacy?"

"What, can't get it up with an audience?" Besty joked.

"Fuck, I'm ready to burst," Pope laughed.

"Okay, don't take too fucking long about it."

Besty walked off towards the office while Pope grabbed me, opened the car door and shoved me inside.

Climbing on top of me, he held me down. "Shhh," he whispered, and then turned his head to see if the coast was clear.

"Stay down," he warned.

I tried to adjust my clothing, but he told me to leave it.

"When did you call them?" I asked eagerly. "What did they say?"

"I phoned them after you asked me. I owe you for Portsmouth."

I recalled the incident where I saved his arse on one of the most violent Hawk runs.

"Who did you talk to?" I asked.

"Don't know his name - some officer of the club," he shrugged.

I hoped to God it wasn't Gbh.

"Look, Gemma. I have to cut and run. I've gotta make this phone call if you're gonna get out of this in one piece."

"You're gonna leave me alone with him," I cried.

"I have to. You've got to hold on, okay? Just don't antagonise the bastard; he's upset with you enough already. Do what he says."

Yes. That seemed the most sensible thing to do. Now that I was going to be rescued, I thought I could cope with what Besty had in mind for me.

"Don't aggravate him," Pope warned as he climbed out of the car. "And take your fucking jeans off," he whispered loudly, "You've supposed to have been raped, remember?"

I nodded and quickly got undressed. I stayed where I was and waited. I just wanted to get it over with. I thought he'd climb into the back and fuck me, but Besty had other plans.

The sickly smile had vanished, replaced now with intense anger. He reached into the car, grabbed my hair and pulled me out, flinging me to the floor. My scream was cut off as a steel cap of his boots found my face. I thought I was going to choke on my own teeth and blood. I wish I'd blacked out then, but I was conscious through the rest of his violent beating. The guy wasn't going to stop. Each pounding first, each kick, was given with such brute force intent on destroying. The last thing I remembered was being thrown across the bonnet of the car.

Road Rage

***

Someone was calling my name. I tried to open my eyes, but it was as though they were glued shut. My eyelashes ripped as I struggled to lift up a lid. I made out a blurred vision of a guy leaning over me. I tried to ask if I came off my bike again but all that came out of my mouth was blood and the sound of nasal grunting. At the time, I didn't know I'd been beaten senseless. I honestly thought I'd been racing and was lying on the road after coming off my bike. I thought I was talking to Blade. It was weird. I wasn't in agony, even though my mind and body were broken. I was in pain, but it was like a frozen pain.

"Doc, calm down," I heard someone yell, but even my hearing was a muffled as my sight.

"Gem needs you. You've got to calm yourself."

The blackness covered me again and it seemed like I was frozen in darkness forever.

***

I was in a coma for two weeks and Doc's face was the first thing I saw when I woke. My jaw was wired shut, my left arm and leg immobilised, and my head felt like a hundred-ton weight. I couldn't move.

My memory was still fogged, my mind muddled, but Doc soon put that right. He told me what happened, and the story I was supposed to give the police.

Blade, Doc and Gbh were already in town looking for the van when they got the call from Pope. Thankfully, Blade used his head and instead of storming the garage with guns blazing, he called the police instead. Doc said Gbh wasn't happy about that. When Rage showed up at the garage, the cops already had Besty in handcuffs.

As far as the police were concerned, I was down south visiting a friend, but because I was openly displaying my colours in another MC's territory, the Hawks grabbed me. I was drugged, and the rest was obvious. Of course, there was no mention of the guns. No evidence that I ever had

149

them.

The story wasn't as far fetched as it seemed, especially as my sliced-up jacket was evidence of the attack and their hate for other motorcycle clubs.

"You know it's not going to look good for you when it comes out that you used to ride with the Hawks," Doc said.

I shrugged my shoulders and then wrote on the writing pad Doc had given me. "Hawks won't say or deny. Besty will take fall not club. He do time and be rewarded. Trip is clean. That's the way it works."

I wasn't about to testify in court and have the Hawks hunting down Rage in retribution, so I knew Trip would walk away from this.

Doc shook his head. "No, Gem, he won't be getting away with it. It's being dealt with."

I tried to scream no, but nothing but a loud muffled groan came out. That didn't stop me from continuing my meaningless noise. Doc tapped the pad, reminding me he couldn't understand what I was trying to say. I was so frustrated; I had so much I wanted to make it clear to him. I gave an angry sigh and then wrote in big letters across the page, "NO NO NO!"

"It's okay," Doc urged. "Rage won't be associated with the hit; we've hired outside help."

Doc assumed that would calm me, but it only made me more agitated. I turned the page of the writing pad and wrote "It will blow back. If Hawks find out, Rage will be hunted down." I gave him the pad, watched him read, and saw the smile on his face.

"Don't worry we've got that part covered. There's is no way that bastard is getting away with what he's done to you. It's taken care of; we've covered our tracks so stop stressing."

He kissed the top of my head. Yes, I was stressing and for good reason. I knew that the only way Trip's murder would not fall back onto to Rage was if they silenced the

Road Rage

hired help. Whoever had taken the contract had sealed their own death warrant.

Besty was charged with my kidnapping assault and rape. Shame the lawyer couldn't pin attempted murder on him because that's what it was. The guy did his best to finish me off, whether it was premeditated or not. I had to assume Rage's plan worked, and Trip was taken care of, but neither Doc nor any of the officers mentioned him again.

***

I still haven't got over what happened. As strong as I thought I was, Trip did what he promised; he broke me in body, mind and spirit. I haven't ridden a bike since. My fearlessness and want for adrenaline had left me completely. I resigned my post as treasurer and, even though I wasn't racing anymore, I was still permitted to wear the Rage patch. After what I'd been through for the club, they owed me. My social butterfly title deflated, as did my ego. I now preferred to stay indoors rather than being down the pub among friends and surrounded by happy vibes. Doc understood my attitude and never pushed me into unwanted situations. Rage did their best to help me forget about what happened, but the way they tiptoed around me, just added to my lack of self-worth.

Thankfully, Blade decided it was too much of a risk to continue selling guns. Our racing team had good standing around the circuit and sponsors were queuing up for us to wear their name. He realised that it would take only one slip to lose it all. I wasn't the only one who was happy with his decision. Doc wanted to get out of the game as well.

The club continued street racing. After all, that's how Rage first started. That's where we made our name and good money.

I still had the courage to get on the back of Doc's bike. My bike, however, was shut in the garage, a home for spiders and dust. I doubted I'd ever have the nerve to ride it again. It wasn't that I was scared of the speed or coming off the bike, I just couldn't cope with anything that increased my adrenaline. Whenever the nerves kicked in and my heart started beating fast, I ended up having a panic attack.

I refused to take the antidepressants Doc offered. I was determined to get past it, no matter how long it took. The therapy I had helped me open up to Doc, to talk about my shameful past, and to accept who I really was. Although I had changed my attitude since riding with the Hawks, I was still the angry, tough person inside. The therapist said that there were two personalities fighting inside of me and if I couldn't decide and agree on which one, I was going to live, I would end up losing it completely and have a mental breakdown. That was the wake-up call I needed.

***

The sky was clear of clouds. The sun shined brightly and even the birds were singing. It was the perfect day. We blocked the road with our bikes, and we didn't care. This was how Rage ran. Dawn looked amazing in her ivory wedding dress. Her hair was pinned up and white roses crowned her head. I'd never seen her in a dress before. Come to think of it, I'd never seen either of them in anything other than jeans and t-shirts. Apart from the bride, groom and Turbo, who was best man, the rest of Rage were in leathers. I had a black dress folded up in a bag under the seat of Doc's bike ready to change into for the reception which was being held at a quaint pub beside the locks.

Dawn was beaming as she walked beside her father through the procession of gleaming super bikes.

We caused quite a commotion on the road. Residents came out of their homes to watch the scene, and a helicopter flew overhead. I wasn't sure if it was the police or a TV crew; either way we didn't care. This was Dawn's and Pat's day, and we wanted it to be special for them. Once Dawn had walked into the church, we parked our bikes and then piled inside.

Doc held my hand while we listened to the priest. And when Pat said, "I do," I squeezed Doc's hand and looked into his face. Doc smiled back at me. The rest of their vows were muffled as I blocked out my surroundings and just stared at the statue of Christ. I knew how lucky I was to be alive, to be standing there with my brothers, watching and being part of this happy occasion. For a few seconds, my life rushed past me. Silent images of the laughter and terror I had faced. I shivered as I fought back my emotions. I think I was waiting for an answer as to why I was still alive, some hint on what was going to happen next. But no answer came and the sound of the church organ warming up woke me from my thoughts.

The ceremony was over quickly and, once the pictures were out of the way, the happy couple rode away on their bike with tin cans clanking behind them.

It was early hours by the time we arrived home. Doc had only a couple of drinks that night, so he was sober enough to ride. I, on the other hand, had gotten through a bottle of champagne and at least four vodkas. I know Doc had been keeping watch on my intake, but I didn't think it was out of hand. Didn't I deserve a drink now and again after what I'd been through?

"Can I ask you something," I said to Doc as we cuddled up together in bed.

"Sure, honey."

I loved it when he called me that.

"What's your real name? Not like I'm gonna start calling you by it, but I'd just like to know."

"It's Colin." He laughed.

"Colin," I repeated. "Sorry, but I don't see you as a Colin. "You'll always be my Doc." I squeezed and kissed his arm.

He pulled me closer. "And you will always be my Gem."

"Can I be honest with you?" I quietly asked.

"I hope we can always be honest with each other," he

replied.

I sat up and turned towards him. "Even though I don't blame Rage for what happened to me, I don't think I can stay here. There's too much history here and I can't try to heal when the memory of what occurred is staring me in the face everywhere I go."

Doc sat up and listened intently while I continued.

"It's too much."

"Did your therapist tell you this?" he asked.

"She mentioned a break would do me good. But I've been thinking about this for a while."

"You always seemed to be running away from your fears," he said.

I turned my head away, but then he gently touched my arm.

"Any other time, I would say stay and deal with it. But I understand where you're coming from. I know how hard it must be for you. You forget I've been with you every step of the way and it's been one hell of a nightmare journey. I may not have been through what you did, but I relive each moment with you every time I close my eyes."

I reached out my hand and caressed his cheek.

He moved my hand to his lips and kissed it softly. "I think it's best if we move away from here. A new start for us."

My eyes widened with surprise. "You mean you'd leave Rage, your job? You'd do that for me?"

"Haven't you realised, honey, I would do anything for you?"

"But why?" I needed him to tell me why I was worth the effort. Why I was special to him.

"Gem, I fell in love with you, the first time I saw you. I knew Shep was wrong for you, but I stupidly stayed out of it. I wish now I'd told you how I felt and asked you out straight away. The truth is I didn't think you'd be interested in someone like me. In the looks department, I'm totally out of Shep's league."

Road Rage

I laughed. "God, I'm not that superficial. I guess I was taken back by Shep's interest in me, and then the way he flirted made me feel good about myself. It had been awhile since I felt attractive."

Doc shook his head. "I wish you could see what other people see. I wish I could see how you see yourself. Why do you always put yourself down? You are beautiful inside and out and I love every part of you. These," he said, running his finger down each side of my face. "These make you who you are today. They are part of you and it's nothing to be ashamed off. You've got to stop thinking about what other people think. You're far too vain. Anyhow, only my opinion counts," he laughed.

Man, I loved that laugh. It was deep and his belly shook as he held me.

"You are my angel," he whispered. "I needed stability in my life, and you came at the right time."

"I haven't done much," I argued, "apart from trashing two of your bikes and causing a right nuisance of myself," I laughed.

"You're wrong there. You've kept me busy, kept me on the straight and narrow. You've given me a purpose again."

Wow, I never knew he felt that way.

"That's why I think it would be good for us to leave all this crap behind. Travel for a while, and then we can decide where to settle down. I've enough savings to last a fair while."

"Sounds perfect," I murmured, as I cuddled his chest.

"It will take a while to organise things. The house needs to go on the market, and I have to give my notice in at work, but we'll leave as soon as we can. Okay, babe?"

"Whatever you say," I replied. "You're the boss."

***

The tropical morning sun warmed the golden sands as I walked barefoot to where Doc waited for me, wearing light brown cotton slacks and a cream shirt and gold-coloured tie. I'd never known him to look so handsome before. I

wanted to imprint the memory of him standing there, with that huge grin on his face.

He held his hand out to me and I took it without hesitation. Drums beat in the rhythm of the chorus as I looked into Doc's face and said. "I do."

<<< THE END >>>

A Note from the Author

To all my readers who have just finished the series, thank you for coming on this journey with me and I hope you enjoyed the ride.

Many thanks for reading this book. Reviews are very important to an author so please take a moment to leave a rating and review.
Thank you so much.

Karina Kantas

More titles by Karina Kantas

The Outlaw Series

In Times of Violence
Huntress
Lawless Justice
Road Rage

Illusional Reality Duology

Illusional Reality
The Quest
Box set
Audio book of Illusional Reality
Illusional Reality the Colouring Book
Illusional Reality Journal

Flash and Short Story Collection

Heads & Tales
Undressed
A Flash of Horror

Stone Cold
Stone Cold Audio book
Toxic
Broken Chains
In Times of Violence YA Edition

Social Media

You can find Karina Kantas on Facebook, Twitter, Instagram, TikTok, MEWE, and Goodreads

www.ingramcontent.com/pod-product-compliance
Lightning Source LLC
Chambersburg PA
CBHW030803190726
48285CB00003B/997